To Florence Thompson
from Mother

June 8th 1916

LAVENDER AND OLD LACE

BY

MYRTLE REED

Author of

"Flower of the Dusk"
"The Master's Violin"
"A Spinner in the Sun"
"At the Sign of the Jack o' Lantern"
Etc.

New York
GROSSET & DUNLAP
Publishers

BY MYRTLE REED:

A Weaver of Dreams	Sonnets to a Lover
Old Rose and Silver	Master of the Vineyard
Lavender and Old Lace	Flower of the Dusk
The Master's Violin	At the Sign of the Jack-o'-Lantern
Love Letters of a Musician	A Spinner in the Sun
The Spinster Book	Later Love Letters of a Musician
The Shadow of Victory	Love Affairs of Literary Men

Myrtle Reed Year Book

This edition is issued under arrangement with the publishers
G. P. PUTNAM'S SONS, NEW YORK AND LONDON

Contents

		PAGE
I.—THE LIGHT IN THE WINDOW	.	1
II.—THE ATTIC	. . . .	22
III.—MISS AINSLIE	. . . .	39
IV.—A GUEST	. . . . .	54
V.—THE RUMOURS OF THE VALLEY	.	67
VI.—THE GARDEN	. . . .	81
VII.—THE MAN WHO HESITATES	. .	98
VIII.—SUMMER DAYS	. . . .	110
IX.—BY HUMBLE MEANS	. . .	125
X.—LOVE LETTERS	. . . .	138
XI.—THE ROSE OF ALL THE WORLD	.	152
XII.—BRIDE AND GROOM	. . .	159
XIII.—PLANS	. . . . .	177
XIV.—"FOR REMEMBRANCE"	. .	199
XV.—THE SECRET AND THE DREAM	.	222
XVI.—SOME ONE WHO LOVED HER	.	241
XVII.—DAWN	. . . . .	254

I

The Light in the Window

A RICKETY carriage was slowly ascending
the hill, and from the place of honour on
the back seat, the single passenger surveyed the
country with interest and admiration.   The
driver of that ancient chariot was an awkward
young fellow, possibly twenty-five years of
age, with sharp knees, large, red hands, high
cheek-bones, and abundant hair of a shade
verging upon orange.   He was not unpleas-
ant to look upon, however, for he had a certain evident honesty, and he was disposed to
be friendly to every one.

"Be you comfortable, Miss?" he asked,
with apparent solicitude.

"Very comfortable, thank you," was the
quiet response.

He urged his venerable steeds to a gait of
about two miles an hour, then turned side-
ways.

"Be you goin' to stay long, Miss?"

"All Summer, I think."

"Do tell!"

The young woman smiled in listless amusement, but Joe took it for conversational encouragement. "City folks is dretful bashful when they's away from home," he said to himself. He clucked again to his unheeding horses, shifted his quid, and was casting about for a new topic when a light broke in upon him.

"I guess, now, that you're Miss Hathaway's niece, what's come to stay in her house while she goes gallivantin' and travellin' in furrin parts, be n't you?"

"I am Miss Hathaway's niece, and I have never been here before. Where does she live?"

"Up yander."

He flourished the discarded fish-pole which served as a whip, and pointed out a small white house on the brow of the hill. Reflection brought him the conviction that his remark concerning Miss Hathaway was a social mistake, since his passenger sat very straight, and asked no more questions.

The weary wheels creaked, but the collapse which Miss Thorne momentarily expected was

mercifully postponed. Being gifted with imagination, she experienced the emotion of a
wreck without bodily harm. As in a photograph, she beheld herself suddenly projected
into space, followed by her suit case, felt her
new hat wrenched from her head, and saw
hopeless gravel stains upon the tailored gown
which was the pride of her heart. She thought
a sprained ankle would be the inevitable out-
come of the fall, but was spared the pain of it,
for the inability to realise an actual hurt is the
redeeming feature of imagination.

Suddenly there was a snort of terror from
one of the horses, and the carriage stopped
abruptly. Ruth clutched her suit case and
umbrella, instantly prepared for the worst;
but Joe reassured her.

"Now don't you go and get skeered, Miss,"
he said, kindly; "'t aint nothin' in the world
but a rabbit. Mamie can't never get used to
rabbits, someways." He indicated one of the
horses—a high, raw-boned animal, sketched
on a generous plan, whose ribs and joints
protruded, and whose rough white coat had
been weather-worn to grey.

"Hush now, Mamie," he said; "'t aint
nothin'."

"Mamie" looked around inquiringly, with one ear erect and the other at an angle. A cataract partially concealed one eye, but in the other was a world of wickedness and knowledge, modified by a certain lady-like reserve.

"G' long, Mamie!"

Ruth laughed as the horse resumed motion in mincing, maidenly steps. "What's the other one's name?" she asked.

"Him? His name's Alfred. Mamie's his mother."

Miss Thorne endeavoured to conceal her amusement and Joe was pleased because the ice was broken. "I change their names every once in a while," he said, "'cause it makes some variety, but now I've named 'em about all the names I know."

The road wound upward in its own lazy fashion, and there were trees at the left, though only one or two shaded the hill itself. As they approached the summit, a girl in a blue gingham dress and a neat white apron came out to meet them.

"Come right in, Miss Thorne," she said, "and I'll explain it to you."

Ruth descended, inwardly vowing that she would ride no more in Joe's carriage, and after giving some directions about her trunk, followed her guide indoors.

The storm-beaten house was certainly entitled to the respect accorded to age. It was substantial, but unpretentious in outline, and had not been painted for a long time. The faded green shutters blended harmoniously with the greyish white background, and the piazza, which was evidently an unhappy afterthought of the architect, had two or three new shingles on its roof.

"You see it's this way, Miss Thorne," the maid began, volubly; "Miss Hathaway, she went earlier than she laid out to, on account of the folks decidin' to take a steamer that sailed beforehand — before the other one, I mean. She went in sech a hurry that she did n't have time to send you word and get an answer, but she's left a letter here for you, for she trusted to your comin'."

Miss Thorne laid her hat and jacket aside and settled herself comfortably in a rocker. The maid returned presently with a letter which Miss Hathaway had sealed with half an ounce of red wax, presumably in a laudable effort to remove temptation from the path of the red-cheeked, wholesome, farmer's daughter

who stood near by with her hands on her
hips.

"Miss Ruth Thorne," the letter began,
"Dear Niece:

"I am writing this in a hurry, as we are
going a week before we expected to. I think
you will find everything all right. Hepsey
will attend to the house-keeping, for I don't
suppose you know much about it, coming
from the city. She's a good-hearted girl, but
she's set in her ways, and you'll have to
kinder give in to her, but any time when you
can't, just speak to her sharp and she'll do as
you tell her.

"I have left money enough for the expenses
until I come back, in a little box on the top
shelf of the closet in the front room, under a
pile of blankets and comfortables. The key
that unlocks it is hung on a nail driven into
the back of the old bureau in the attic. I believe Hepsey is honest and reliable, but I don't
believe in tempting folks.

"When I get anywhere where I can, I will
write and send you my address, and then you
can tell me how things are going at home.
The catnip is hanging from the rafters in the

attic, in case you should want some tea, and the sassafras is in the little drawer in the bureau that's got the key hanging behind it.

"If there's anything else you should want, I reckon Hepsey will know where to find it. Hoping that this will find you enjoying the great blessing of good health, I remain,

"Your Affectionate Aunt,

"JANE HATHAWAY.

"P. S. You have to keep a lamp burning every night in the east window of the attic. Be careful that nothing catches afire."

The maid was waiting, in fear and trembling, for she did not know what directions her eccentric mistress might have left. "Everything is all right, Hepsey," said Miss Thorne, pleasantly, "and I think you and I will get along nicely. Did Miss Hathaway tell you what room I was to have?"

"No'm. She told me you was to make yourself at home. She said you could sleep where you pleased."

"Very well, I will go up and see for myself. I would like my tea at six o'clock."

She still held the letter in her hand, greatly to the chagrin of Hepsey, who was intereste in everything and had counted upon a peep at it. It was not Miss Hathaway's custom to guard her letters and she was both surprised and disappointed.

As Ruth climbed the narrow stairway, the quiet, old-fashioned house brought balm to her tired soul. It was exquisitely clean, redolent of sweet herbs, and in its atmosphere was a subtle, Puritan restraint.

Have not our houses, mute as they are, their own way of conveying an impression? One may go into a house which has been empty for a long time, and yet feel, instinctively, what sort of people were last sheltered there. The silent walls breathe a message to each visitor, and as the footfalls echo in the bare, cheerless rooms, one discovers where Sorrow and Trouble had their abode, and where the light, careless laughter of gay Bohemia lingered until dawn. At night, who has not heard ghostly steps upon the stairs, the soft closing of unseen doors, the tapping on a window, and, perchance, a sigh or the sound of tears? Timid souls may shudder and be afraid, but wiser folk smile, with reminiscent tenderness, when the old house dreams.

As she wandered through the tiny, spotless

rooms on the second floor of Miss Hathaway's
house, Ruth had a sense of security and peace
which she had never known before. There
were two front rooms, of equal size, looking
to the west, and she chose the one on the
left, because of its two south windows.
There was but one other room, aside from the
small one at the end of the hall, which, as she
supposed, was Hepsey's.

One of the closets was empty, but on a shelf
in the other was a great pile of bedding. She
dragged a chair inside, burrowed under the
blankets, and found a small wooden box, the
contents clinking softly as she drew it toward
her.

Holding it under her arm, she ascended the
narrow, spiral stairs which led to the attic.
At one end, under the eaves, stood an old
mahogany dresser. The casters were gone
and she moved it with difficulty, but the slant-
ing sunbeams of late afternoon revealed the
key, which hung, as her aunt had written, on
a nail driven into the back of it.

She knew, without trying, that it would fit
the box, but idly turned the lock. As she
opened it, a bit of paper fluttered out, and,
picking it up, she read in her aunt's cramped,

but distinct hand: "Hepsey gets a dollar and a half every week. Don't you pay her no more."

As the house was set some distance back, the east window in the attic was the only one which commanded a view of the sea. A small table, with its legs sawed off, came exactly to the sill, and here stood a lamp, which was a lamp simply, without adornment, and held about a pint of oil.

She read the letter again and, having mastered its contents, tore it into small pieces, with that urban caution which does not come amiss in the rural districts. She understood that every night of her stay she was to light this lamp with her own hands, but why? The varnish on the table, which had once been glaring, was scratched with innumerable rings, where the rough glass had left its mark. Ruth wondered if she were face to face with a mystery.

The seaward side of the hill was a rocky cliff, and between the vegetable garden at the back of the house and the edge of the Precipice were a few stumps, well-nigh covered with moss. From her vantage point, she could see the woods which began at the base of the hill, on the north side, and seemed to end at the sea. On the south, there were a few trees near the cliff, but others near them had been cut down.

Still farther south and below the hill was a grassy plain, through which a glistening river wound slowly to the ocean. Willows grew along its margin, tipped with silvery green, and with masses of purple twilight tangled in the bare branches below.

Ruth opened the window and drew a long breath. Her senses had been dulled by the years in the city, but childhood, hidden though not forgotten, came back as if by magic, with that first scent of sea and Spring.

As yet, she had not fully realised how grateful she was for this little time away from her desk and typewriter. The managing editor had promised her the same position, whenever she chose to go back, and there was a little hoard in the savings-bank, which she would not need to touch, owing to the kindness of this eccentric aunt, whom she had never seen.

The large room was a typical attic, with its spinning-wheel and discarded furniture—colonial mahogany that would make many a

city matron envious, and for which its owner
cared little or nothing. There were chests
of drawers, two or three battered trunks, a
cedar chest, and countless boxes, of various
sizes. Bunches of sweet herbs hung from the
rafters, but there were no cobwebs, because
of Miss Hathaway's perfect housekeeping.

Ruth regretted the cobwebs and decided
not to interfere, should the tiny spinners take
advantage of Aunt Jane's absence. She found
an old chair which was unsteady on its rockers
but not yet depraved enough to betray one's
confidence. Moving it to the window, she
sat down and looked out at the sea, where
the slow boom of the surf came softly from
the shore, mingled with the liquid melody
of returning breakers.

The first grey of twilight had come upon
the world before she thought of going downstairs. A match-safe hung upon the window
casing, newly filled, and, mindful of her trust,
she lighted the lamp and closed the window.
Then a sudden scream from the floor below
startled her.

"Miss Thorne! Miss Thorne!" cried a
shrill voice. "Come here! Quick!"

White as a sheet, Ruth flew downstairs

and met Hepsey in the hall. "What on earth is the matter!" she gasped.

"Joe's come with your trunk," responded that volcanic young woman, amiably; "where'd you want it put?"

"In the south front room," she answered, still frightened, but glad nothing more serious had happened. "You mustn't scream like that."

"Supper's ready," resumed Hepsey, nonchalantly, and Ruth followed her down to the little dining-room.

As she ate, she plied the maid with questions. "Does Miss Hathaway light that lamp in the attic every night?"

"Yes'm. She cleans it and fills it herself, and she puts it out every morning. She don't never let me touch it."

"Why does she keep it there?"

"D' know. She d' know, neither."

"Why, Hepsey, what do you mean? Why does she do it if she doesn't know why she does it?"

"D' know. 'Cause she wants to, I reckon."

"She's been gone a week, hasn't she?"

"No'm. Only six days. It'll be a week to-morrer."

Hepsey's remarks were short and jerky, as a rule, and had a certain explosive force.

"Has n't the lamp been lighted since she went away?"

"Yes 'm. I was to do it till you come, and after you got here I was to ask you every night if you 'd forgot it."

Ruth smiled because Aunt Jane's old-fashioned exactness lingered in her wake. "Now see here, Hepsey," she began kindly, "I don 't know and you don 't know, but I 'd like to have you tell me what you think about it."

"I d' know, as you say, mum, but I think —" here she lowered her voice — "I think it has something to do with Miss Ainslie."

"Who is Miss Ainslie?"

"She 's a peculiar woman, Miss Ainslie is," the girl explained, smoothing her apron, "and she lives down the road a piece, in the valley as you may say. She don 't never go no-wheres, Miss Ainslie don 't, but folks goes to see her. She 's got a funny house—I 've been inside of it sometimes when I 've been down on errands for Miss Hathaway. She ain't got no figgered wall paper, nor no lace curtains, and she ain't got no rag carpets neither. Her

floors is all kinder funny, and she's got
heathen things spread down onto 'em. Her
house is full of heathen things, and sometimes
she wears 'em."

"Wears what, Hepsey? The 'heathen
things' in the house?"

"No'm. Other heathen things she's got
put away somewheres. She's got money, I
guess, but she's got furniture in her parlour
that's just like what Miss Hathaway's got set
away in the attic. We would n't use them
kind of things, nohow," she added compla-
cently.

"Does she live all alone?"

"Yes'm. Joe, he does her errands and
other folks stops in sometimes, but Miss
Ainslie ain't left her front yard for I d' know
how long. Some says she's cracked, but she's
the best housekeeper round here, and if she
hears of anybody that's sick or in trouble, she
allers sends 'em things. She ain't never been
up here, but Miss Hathaway, she goes down
there sometimes, and she 'n Miss Ainslie
swaps cookin' quite regler. I have to go
down there with a plate of somethin' Miss
Hathaway's made, and Miss Ainslie allers
says: 'Wait just a moment, please, Hepsey, I

would like to send Miss Hathaway a jar of my preserves.'"

She relapsed unconsciously into imitation of Miss Ainslie's speech. In the few words, softened, and betraying a quaint stateliness, Ruth caught a glimpse of an old-fashioned gentlewoman, reserved and yet gracious.

She folded her napkin, saying: "You make the best biscuits I ever tasted, Hepsey." The girl smiled, but made no reply.

"What makes you think Miss Ainslie has anything to do with the light?" she inquired after a little.

"'Cause there wasn't no light in that winder when I first come—leastways, not as I know of—and after I'd been here a week or so, Miss Hathaway, she come back from there one day looking kinder strange. She didn't say much; but the next mornin' she goes down to town and buys that lamp, and she saws off them table legs herself. Every night since, that light's been a-goin', and she puts it out herself every mornin' before she comes downstairs."

"Perhaps she and Miss Ainslie had been talking of shipwreck, and she thought she would have a little lighthouse of her own,"

Miss Thorne suggested, when the silence became oppressive.

"P'raps so," rejoined Hepsey.   She had become stolid again.

Ruth pushed her chair back and stood at the dining-room window a moment, looking out into the yard.   The valley was in shadow, but the last light still lingered on the hill. "What's that, Hepsey?" she asked.

"What's what?"

"That—where the evergreen is coming up out of the ground, in the shape of a square."

"That's the cat's grave, mum.   She died jest afore Miss Hathaway went away, and she planted the evergreen."

"I thought something was lacking," said Ruth, half to herself.

"Do you want a kitten, Miss Thorne?" inquired Hepsey, eagerly.   "I reckon I can get you one—Maltese or white, just as you like."

"No, thank you, Hepsey; I don't believe I'll import any pets."

"Jest as you say, mum.   It's sorter lonesome, though, with no cat; and Miss Hathaway said she did n't want no more."

Speculating upon the departed cat's superior charms, that made substitution seem like sacrilege to Miss Hathaway, Ruth sat down for a time in the old-fashioned parlour, where the shabby haircloth furniture was ornamented with "tidies" to the last degree. There was a marble-topped centre table in the room, and a basket of wax flowers under a glass case, Mrs. Hemans's poems, another book, called *The Lady's Garland,* and the family Bible were carefully arranged upon it.

A hair wreath, also sheltered by glass, hung on the wall near another collection of wax flowers suitably framed. There were various portraits of people whom Miss Thorne did not know, though she was a near relative of their owner, and two tall, white china vases, decorated with gilt, flanked the mantel-shelf. The carpet, which was once of the speaking variety, had faded to the listening point. Coarse lace curtains hung from brass rings on wooden poles, and red cotton lambrequins were festooned at the top.

Hepsey came in to light the lamp that hung by chains over the table, but Miss Thorne rose, saying: "You need n't mind, Hepsey, as I am going upstairs."

"Want me to help you unpack?" she asked, doubtless wishing for a view of "city clothes."

"No, thank you."

"I put a pitcher of water in your room, Miss Thorne. Is there anything else you would like?"

"Nothing more, thank you."

She still lingered, irresolute, shifting from one foot to the other. "Miss Thorne—" she began hesitatingly.

"Yes?"

"Be you—be you a lady detective?"

Ruth's clear laughter rang out on the evening air. "Why, no, you foolish girl; I'm a newspaper woman, and I've earned a rest — that's all. You must n't read books with yellow covers."

Hepsey withdrew, muttering vague apologies, and Ruth found her at the head of the stairs when she went up to her room. "How long have you been with Miss Hathaway?" she asked.

"Five years come next June."

"Good night, Hepsey."

"Good night, Miss Thorne."

From sheer force of habit, Ruth locked her door. Her trunk was not a large one, and it did not take her long to put her simple wardrobe into the capacious closet and the dresser drawers.   As she moved the empty trunk into the closet, she remembered the box of money that she had left in the attic, and went up to get it.   When she returned she heard Hepsey's door close softly.

"Silly child," she said to herself.   "I might just as well ask her if she is n't a 'lady detective.'   They 'll laugh about that in the office when I go back."

She sat down, rocking contentedly, for it was April, and she would not have to go back until Aunt Jane came home, probably about the first of October.   She checked off the free, health-giving months on her tired fingers, that would know the blue pencil and the type-writer no more until Autumn, when she would be strong again and the quivering nerves quite steady.

She blessed the legacy which had fallen into Jane Hathaway's lap and led her, at fifty-five, to join a " personally conducted " party to the Old World.   Ruth had always had a dim yearning for foreign travel, but just now she felt no latent injustice, such as had often ran-kled in her soul when her friends went and she remained at home.

Thinking she heard Hepsey in the hall, and

not caring to arouse further suspicion, she put out her light and sat by the window, with the shutters wide open.

Far down the hill, where the road became level again, and on the left as she looked toward the village, was the white house, surrounded by a garden and a hedge, which she supposed was Miss Ainslie's. A timid chirp came from the grass, and the faint, sweet smell of growing things floated in through the open window at the other end of the room.

A train from the city sounded a warning whistle as it approached the station, and then a light shone on the grass in front of Miss Ainslie's house. It was a little gleam, evidently from a candle.

"So she's keeping a lighthouse, too," thought Ruth. The train pulled out of the station and half an hour afterward the light disappeared.

She meditated upon the general subject of illumination while she got ready for bed, but as soon as her head touched the pillow she lost consciousness and knew no more until the morning light crept into her room.

II

The Attic

THE maid sat in the kitchen, wondering why Miss Thorne did not come down. It was almost seven o'clock, and Miss Hathaway's breakfast hour was half past six. Hepsey did not frame the thought, but she had a vague impression that the guest was lazy.

Yet she was grateful for the new interest which had come into her monotonous life. Affairs moved like clock work at Miss Hathaway's — breakfast at half past six, dinner at one, and supper at half past five. Each day was also set apart by its regular duties, from the washing on Monday to the baking on Saturday.

Now it was possible that there might be a change. Miss Thorne seemed fully capable of setting the house topsy-turvy — and Miss Hathaway's last injunction had been: "Now,

Hepsey, you mind Miss Thorne. If I hear that you don't, you 'll lose your place."

The young woman who slumbered peacefully upstairs, while the rest of the world was awake, had, from the beginning, aroused admiration in Hepsey's breast. It was a reluctant, rebellious feeling, mingled with an indefinite fear, but it was admiration none the less.

During the greater part of a wondering, wakeful night, the excited Hepsey had seen Miss Thorne as plainly as when she first entered the house. The tall, straight, graceful figure was familiar by this time, and the subdued silken rustle of her skirts was a wonted sound. Ruth's face, naturally mobile, had been schooled into a certain reserve, but her deep, dark eyes were eloquent, and always would be. Hepsey wondered at the opaque whiteness of her skin and the baffling arrangement of her hair. The young women of the village had rosy cheeks, but Miss Thorne's face was colourless, except for her lips.

It was very strange, Hepsey thought, for Miss Hathaway to sail before her niece came, if, indeed, Miss Thorne was her niece. There was a mystery in the house on the hilltop,

which she had tried in vain to fathom. Foreign
letters came frequently, no two of them from
the same person, and the lamp in the attic
window had burned steadily every night for
five years. Otherwise, everything was ex-
plainable and sane.

Still, Miss Thorne did not seem even re-
motely related to her aunt, and Hepsey had
her doubts. Moreover, the guest had an un-
canny gift which amounted to second sight.
How did she know that all of Hepsey's books
had yellow covers? Miss Hathaway could not
have told her in the letter, for the mistress was
not aware of her maid's literary tendencies.

It was half past seven, but no sound came
from upstairs. She replenished the fire and
resumed meditation. Whatever Miss Thorne
might prove to be, she was decidedly interesting. It was pleasant to watch her, to feel the
subtle refinement of all her belongings, and to
wonder what was going to happen next.
Perhaps Miss Thorne would take her back to
the city, as her maid, when Miss Hathaway
came home, for, in the books, such things
frequently happened. Would she go? Hepsey was trying to decide, when there was a
light, rapid step on the stairs, a moment's

hesitation in the hall, and Miss Thorne came into the dining-room.

"Good morning, Hepsey," she said, cheerily; "am I late?"

"Yes 'm. It's goin' on eight, and Miss Hathaway allers has breakfast at half past six."

"How ghastly," Ruth thought. "I should have told you," she said, "I will have mine at eight."

"Yes 'm," replied Hepsey, apparently unmoved. "What time do you want dinner?"

"At six o'clock — luncheon at half past one."

Hepsey was puzzled, but in a few moments she understood that dinner was to be served at night and supper at midday. Breakfast had already been moved forward an hour and a half, and stranger things might happen at any minute.

Ruth had several other reforms in mind, but deemed it best to wait. After breakfast, she remembered the lamp in the window and went up to put it out.

It was still burning when she reached it, though the oil was almost gone, and, placing it by the stairway, that she might not forget to have it filled, she determined to explore the attic to her heart's content.

The sunlight streamed through the east window and searched the farthest corners of the room. The floor was bare and worn, but carefully swept, and the things that were stored there were huddled together far back under the eaves, as if to make room for others.

It was not idle curiosity, but delicate sentiment, that made Ruth eager to open the trunks and dresser drawers, and to turn over the contents of the boxes that were piled together and covered with dust. The interest of the lower part of the house paled in comparison with the first real attic she had ever been in.

After all, why not? Miss Hathaway was her aunt,— her mother's only sister,— and the house was in her care. There was no earthly reason why she should not amuse herself in her own way. Ruth's instincts were against it, but Reason triumphed.

The bunches of dried herbs, hanging from the rafters and swaying back and forth in ghostly fashion, gave out a wholesome fragrance, and when she opened trunks whose

lids creaked on their rusty hinges, dried rosemary, lavender, and sweet clover filled the
room with that long-stored sweetness which
is the gracious handmaiden of Memory.

Miss Hathaway was a thrifty soul, but she
never stored discarded clothing that might be
of use to any one, and so Ruth found no
moth-eaten garments of bygone pattern, but
only things which seemed to be kept for the
sake of their tender associations.

There were letters, on whose yellowed
pages the words had long since faded, a dog-
eared primer, and several well worn school-
books, each having on its fly-leaf: "Jane
Hathaway, Her Book"; scraps of lace, brocade and rustling taffeta, quilt patterns, needle-
books, and all of the eloquent treasures that
a well stored attic can yield.

As she replaced them, singing softly to herself, a folded newspaper slipped to the floor.
It was yellow and worn, like the letters, and
she unfolded it carefully. It was over thirty
years old, and around a paragraph on the
last page a faint line still lingered. It was an
announcement of the marriage of Charles G.
Winfield, captain of the schooner *Mary,* to
Miss Abigail Weatherby.

"Abigail Weatherby," she said aloud. The
name had a sweet, old-fashioned sound.
"They must have been Aunt Jane's friends."
She closed the trunk and pushed it back to its
place, under the eaves.

In a distant corner was the old cedar chest,
heavily carved. She pulled it out into the
light, her cheeks glowing with quiet happiness, and sat down on the floor beside it. It
was evidently Miss Hathaway's treasure box,
put away in the attic when spinsterhood was
confirmed by the fleeting years.

On top, folded carefully in a sheet, was a
gown of white brocade, short-waisted and
quaint, trimmed with pearl passementerie.
The neck was square, cut modestly low, and
filled in with lace of a delicate, frosty pattern
—Point d'Alençon. Underneath the gown
lay piles of lingerie, all of the finest linen,
daintily made by hand. Some of it was
trimmed with real lace, some with crocheted
edging, and the rest with hemstitched ruffles
and feather-stitching.

There was another gown, much worn, of
soft blue cashmere, some sea-shells, a necklace
of uncut turquoises, the colour changed to
green, a prayer-book, a little hymnal, and a

bundle of letters, tied with a faded blue ribbon, which she did not touch. There was but one picture — an ambrotype, in an ornate case, of a handsome young man, with that dashing, dare-devil look in his eyes which has ever been attractive to women.

Ruth smiled as she put the treasures away, thinking that, had Fate thrown the dice another way, the young man might have been her esteemed and respected uncle. Then, all at once, it came to her that she had unthinkingly stumbled upon her aunt's romance.

She was not a woman to pry into others secrets, and felt guilty as she fled from the attic, taking the lamp with her. Afterward, as she sat on the narrow piazza, basking in the warm Spring sunshine, she pieced out the love affair of Jane Hathaway's early girlhood after her own fashion.

She could see it all plainly. Aunt Jane had expected to be married to the dashing young man and had had her trousseau in readiness, when something happened. The folded paper would indicate that he was Charles Winfield, who had married some one else, but whether Aunt Jane had broken her engagement, or the possible Uncle Charles had simply taken a mate

without any such formality, was a subject of
conjecture.

Still, if the recreant lover had married
another, would Aunt Jane have kept her
treasure chest and her wedding gown? Ruth
knew that she herself would not, but she
understood that aunts were in a class by themselves. It was possible that Charles Winfield
was an earlier lover, and she had kept the
paper without any special motive, or, perhaps, for "auld lang syne."

Probably the letters would have disclosed
the mystery, and the newspaper instinct, on
the trail of a "story," was struggling with her
sense of honour, but not for the world, now
that she knew, would Ruth have read the
yellowed pages, which doubtless held faded
roses pressed between them.

The strings of sea-shells, and the larger ones,
which could have come only from foreign
shores, together with the light in the window,
gave her a sudden clew. Aunt Jane was
waiting for her lover and the lamp was a signal. If his name was Charles Winfield, the
other woman was dead, and if not, the marriage notice was that of a friend or an earlier
lover.

The explanation was reasonable, clear, and concise — what woman could ask for more? Yet there was something beyond it which was out of Miss Thorne's grasp — a tantalising something, which would not be allayed. Then she reflected that the Summer was before her, and, in reality, now that she was off the paper, she had no business with other people's affairs.

The sun was hidden by gathering clouds and the air was damp before Ruth missed the bright warmth on the piazza, and began to walk back and forth by way of keeping warm. A gravelled path led to the gate and on either side was a row of lilac bushes, the bare stalks tipped with green. A white picket fence surrounded the yard, except at the back, where the edge of the precipice made it useless. The place was small and well kept, but there were no flower beds except at the front of the house, and there were only two or three trees.

She walked around the vegetable garden at the back of the house, where a portion of her Summer sustenance was planted, and discovered an unused gate at the side, which swung back and forth, idly, without latching. She was looking over the fence and down the steep hillside, when a sharp voice at her elbow made her jump.

"Sech as wants dinner can come in and get it," announced Hepsey, sourly. "I've yelled and yelled till I've most bust my throat and I ain't a-goin' to yell no more."

She returned to the house, a picture of offended dignity, but carefully left the door ajar for Ruth, who discovered, upon this rude awakening from her reverie, that she was very hungry.

In the afternoon, the chill fog made it impossible to go out, for the wind had risen from the sea and driven the salt mist inland. Miss Hathaway's library was meagre and uninteresting, Hepsey was busy in the kitchen, and Ruth was frankly bored. Reduced at last to the desperate strait of putting all her belongings in irreproachable order, she found herself, at four o'clock, without occupation. The temptation in the attic wrestled strongly with her, but she would not go.

It seemed an age until six o'clock. "This won't do," she said to herself; "I'll have to learn how to sew, or crochet, or make tatting. At last, I am to be domesticated. I used to wonder how women had time for the endless fancy work, but I see, now."

She was accustomed to self analysis and introspection, and began to consider what she could get out of the next six months in the way of gain. Physical strength, certainly, but what else ? The prospect was gloomy just then.

"It's goin' to rain, Miss Thorne," said Hepsey, at the door. "Is all the winders shut ?"

"Yes, I think so," she answered.

"Supper's ready any time you want it."

"Very well, I will come now."

When she sat down in the parlour, after doing scant justice to Hepsey's cooking, it was with a grim resignation, of the Puritan sort which, supposedly, went with the house. There was but one place in all the world where she would like to be, and she was afraid to trust herself in the attic.

By an elaborate mental process, she convinced herself that the cedar chest and the old trunks did not concern her in the least, and tried to develop a feminine fear of mice, which was not natural to her. She had just placed herself loftily above all mundane things, when

Hepsey marched into the room, and placed
the attic lamp, newly filled, upon the marble
table.

Here was a manifest duty confronting a very
superior person and, as she went upstairs, she
determined to come back immediately, but
when she had put the light in the seaward
window, she lingered, under the spell of the
room.

The rain beat steadily upon the roof and
dripped from the eaves. The light made dis-
torted shadows upon the wall and floor, while
the bunches of herbs, hanging from the rafters,
swung lightly back and forth when the wind
rattled the windows and shook the old house.

The room seemed peopled by the previous
generation, that had slept in the massive mahogany bed, rocked in the chairs, with sewing or gossip, and stood before the old dresser
on tiptoe, peering eagerly into the mirror
which probably had hung above it. It was as
if Memory sat at the spinning-wheel, idly
twisting the thread, and bringing visions of
the years gone by.

A cracked mirror hung against the wall and
Ruth saw her reflection dimly, as if she, too,
belonged to the ghosts of the attic. She was

not vain, but she was satisfied with her eyes
and hair, her white skin, impervious to tan or
burn, and the shape of her mouth. The saucy
little upward tilt at the end of her nose was
a great cross to her, however, because it was
at variance with the dignified bearing which
she chose to maintain. As she looked, she
wondered, vaguely, if she, like Aunt Jane,
would grow to a loveless old age. It seemed
probable, for, at twenty-five, The Prince had
not appeared. She had her work and was
happy; yet unceasingly, behind those dark
eyes, Ruth's soul kept maidenly watch for its
mate.

When she turned to go downstairs, a folded
newspaper on the floor attracted her attention.
It was near one of the trunks which she had
opened and must have fallen out. She picked
it up, to replace it, but it proved to be another
paper dated a year later than the first one.
There was no marked paragraph, but she soon
discovered the death notice of "Abigail Winfield, *née* Weatherby, aged twenty-two."

She put it into the trunk out of which she
knew it must have fallen, and stood there,
thinking. Those faded letters, hidden under
Aunt Jane's wedding gown, were tempting

her with their mute secret as never before. She hesitated, took three steps toward the cedar chest, then fled ingloriously from the field.

Whoever Charles Winfield was, he was free to love and marry again. Perhaps there had been an estrangement and it was he for whom Aunt Jane was waiting, since sometimes, out of bitterness, the years distil forgiveness. She wondered at the nature which was tender enough to keep the wedding gown and the pathetic little treasures, brave enough to keep the paper, with its evidence of falseness, and great enough to forgive.

Yet, what right had she to suppose Aunt Jane was waiting? Had she gone abroad to seek him and win his recreant heart again? Or was Abigail Weatherby her girlhood friend, who had married unhappily, and then died?

Somewhere in Aunt Jane's fifty-five years there was a romance, but, after all, it was not her niece's business. "I'm an imaginative goose," Ruth said to herself. "I'm asked to keep a light in the window, presumably as an incipient lighthouse, and I've found some old clothes and two old papers in the attic—that's all—and I've constructed a tragedy."

She resolutely put the whole matter aside, as she sat in her room, rocking pensively. Her own lamp had not been filled and was burning dimly, so she put it out and sat in the darkness, listening to the rain.

She had not closed the shutters and did not care to lean out in the storm, and so it was that, when the whistle of the ten o'clock train sounded hoarsely, she saw the little glimmer of light from Miss Ainslie's window, making a faint circle in the darkness. Half an hour later, as before, it was taken away.

The scent of lavender and sweet clover clung to Miss Hathaway's linen, and, insensibly soothed, Ruth went to sleep. After hours of dreamless slumber, she thought she heard a voice calling her and telling her not to forget the light. It was so real that she started to her feet, half expecting to find some one standing beside her.

The rain had ceased, and two or three stars, like timid children, were peeping at the world from behind the threatening cloud. It was that mystical moment which no one may place—the turning of night to day. Far down the hill, ghostly, but not forbidding, was Miss Ainslie's house, the garden around it lying whitely beneath the dews of dawn, and up in the attic window the light still shone, like unfounded hope in a woman's soul, harking across distant seas of misunderstanding and gloom, with its pitiful "All Hail!"

III

Miss Ainslie

RUTH began to feel a lively interest in her Aunt Jane, and to regret that she had not arrived in time to make her acquaintance. She knew that Miss Hathaway was three or four years younger than Mrs. Thorne would have been, had she lived, and that a legacy had recently come to her from an old friend, but that was all, aside from the discoveries in the attic.

She contemplated the crayon portraits in the parlour and hoped she was not related to any of them. In the family album she found no woman whom she would have liked for an aunt, but was determined to know the worst.

"Is Miss Hathaway's picture here, Hepsey?" she asked.

"No 'm. Miss Hathaway, she would n't have her picter in the parlour, nohow. Some folks does, but Miss Hathaway says 't 'aint modest."

"I think she's right, Hepsey," laughed Ruth, "though I never thought of it in just that way. I'll have to wait until she comes home."

In the afternoon she donned the short skirt and heavy shoes of her "office rig," and started down hill to explore the village. It was a day to tempt one out of doors,—cool and bright, with that indefinable crispness which belongs to Spring.

The hill rose sheer from the highlands, which sloped to the river on the left, as she went down, and on the right to the forest. A side path into the woods made her hesitate for a moment, but she went straight on.

It was the usual small town, which nestles at the foot of a hill and eventually climbs over it, through the enterprise of its wealthier residents, but, save for Miss Hathaway's house, the enterprise had not, as yet, become evident. At the foot of the hill, on the left, was Miss Ainslie's house and garden, and directly opposite, with the width of the hill between them, was a brown house, with a lawn, but no garden except that devoted to vegetables.

As she walked through the village, stopping to look at the display of merchandise in the window of the single shop, which was also post-office and grocery, she attracted a great deal of respectful attention, for, in this community, strangers were an event. Ruth reflected that the shop had only to grow to about fifty times its present size in order to become a full-fledged department store and bring upon the town the rank and dignity of a metropolis.

When she turned her face homeward, she had reached the foot of the hill before she realised that the first long walk over country roads was hard for one accustomed to city pavements. A broad, flat stone offered an inviting resting-place, and she sat down, in the shadow of Miss Ainslie's hedge, hoping Joe would pass in time to take her to the top of the hill. The hedge was high and except for the gate the garden was secluded.

"I seem to get more tired every minute," she thought. "I wonder if I've got the rheumatism."

She scanned the horizon eagerly for the dilapidated conveyance which she had once both feared and scorned. No sound could have been more welcome than the rumble of those creaking wheels, nor any sight more pleasing than the conflicting expressions in " Mamie's " single useful eye. She sat there a long time, waiting for deliverance, but it did not come.

" I'll get an alpenstock," she said to herself, as she rose, wearily, and tried to summon courage to start. Then the gate clicked softly and the sweetest voice in the world said: " My dear, you are tired — won't you come in ? "

Turning, she saw Miss Ainslie, smiling graciously. In a moment she had explained that she was Miss Hathaway's niece and that she would be very glad to come in for a few moments.

" Yes," said the sweet voice again, " I know who you are. Your aunt told me all about you and I trust we shall be friends."

Ruth followed her up the gravelled path to the house, and into the parlour, where a wood fire blazed cheerily upon the hearth. " It is so damp this time of year," she went on, "that I like to keep my fire burning."

While they were talking, Ruth's eyes rested with pleasure upon her hostess. She herself was tall, but Miss Ainslie towered above her. She was a woman of poise and magnificent bearing, and she had the composure which comes to some as a right and to others with long social training.

Her abundant hair was like spun silver — it was not merely white, but it shone. Her skin was as fresh and fair as a girl's, and when she smiled, one saw that her teeth were white and even; but the great charm of her face was her eyes. They were violet, so deep in colour as to seem almost black in certain lights, and behind them lay an indescribable something which made Ruth love her instinctively. She might have been forty, or seventy, but she was beautiful, with the beauty that never fades.

At intervals, not wishing to stare, Ruth glanced around the room. Having once seen the woman, one could not fail to recognise her house, for it suited her. The floors were hardwood, highly polished, and partly covered with rare Oriental rugs. The walls were a soft, dark green, bearing no disfiguring design, and the windows were draped with net, edged with Duchesse lace. Miss Hathaway's curtains hung straight to the floor, but Miss Ainslie's were tied back with white cord. The furniture was colonial mahogany, unspoiled by varnish, and rubbed until it shone.

"You have a beautiful home," said Ruth, during a pause.

"Yes," she replied, "I like it."

"You have a great many beautiful things."

"Yes," she answered softly, "they were given to me by a — a friend."

"She must have had a great many," observed Ruth, admiring one of the rugs.

A delicate pink suffused Miss Ainslie's face. "My friend," she said, with quiet dignity, "is a seafaring gentleman."

That explained the rugs, Ruth thought, and the vase, of finest Cloisonné, which stood upon the mantel-shelf. It accounted also for the bertha of Mechlin lace, which was fastened to Miss Ainslie's gown, of lavender cashmere, by a large amethyst inlaid with gold and surrounded by baroque pearls.

For some little time, they talked of Miss Hathaway and her travels. "I told her she was too old to go," said Miss Ainslie, smiling, "but she assured me that she could take care of herself, and I think she can. Even if she couldn't, she is perfectly safe. These 'personally conducted' parties are by far the best, if one goes alone, for the first time."

Ruth knew that, but she was surp ed, nevertheless. "Won't you tell me about my aunt, Miss Ainslie?" she asked. "You know I 've never seen her."

"Why, yes, of course I will! Where shall I begin?"

"At the beginning," answered Ruth, with a little laugh.

"The beginning is very far away, deary," said Miss Ainslie, and Ruth fancied she heard a sigh. "She came here long before I did, and we were girls together. She lived in the old house at the top of the hill, with her father and mother, and I lived here with mine. We were very intimate for a long time, and then we had a quarrel, about something that was so silly and foolish that I cannot even remember what it was. For five years — no, for almost six, we passed each other like strangers, because each was too proud and stubborn to yield. But death, and trouble, brought us together again."

"Who spoke first," asked Ruth, much interested, "you or Aunt Jane?"

"It was I, of course. I don't believe she would have done it. She was always stronger than I, and though I can't remember the cause

of the quarrel, I can feel the hurt to my pride,
even at this day."

"I know," answered Ruth, quickly, "something of the same kind once happened to me,
only it was n't pride that held me back — it
was just plain stubbornness. Sometimes I am
conscious of two selves — one of me is a nice,
polite person that I'm really fond of, and the
other is so contrary and so mulish that I'm
actually afraid of her. When the two come in
conflict the stubborn one always wins. I'm
sorry, but I can't help it."

"Don't you think we're all like that?"
asked Miss Ainslie, readily understanding. "I
do not believe any one can have strength of
character without being stubborn. To hold
one's position in the face of obstacles, and
never be tempted to yield — to me, that seems
the very foundation."

"Yes, but to be unable to yield when you
know you should — that's awful."

"Is it?' inquired Miss Ainslie, with quiet
amusement.

"Ask Aunt Jane," returned Ruth, laughing.
"I begin to perceive our definite relationship."

Miss Ainslie leaned forward to put another
maple log on the fire. "Tell me more about

Aunt Jane," Ruth suggested. "I'm getting to be somebody's relative, instead of an orphan, stranded on the shore of the world."

"She's hard to analyse," began the older woman. "I have never been able to reconcile her firmness with her softness. She's as hard as New England granite, but I think she wears it like a mask. Sometimes, one sees through. She scolds me very often, about anything that occurs to her, but I never pay any attention to it. She says I shouldn't live here all alone, and that I deserve to have something dreadful happen to me, but she had all the trees cut down that stood on the hill between her window and mine, and had a key made to my lower door, and made me promise that if I was ill at any time, I would put a signal in my window — a red shawl in the daytime and a light at night. I hadn't any red shawl and she gave me hers.

"One night — I shall never forget it — I had a terrible attack of neuralgia, during the worst storm I have ever known. I didn't even know that I put the light in the window — I was so beside myself with pain — but she came, at two o'clock in the morning, and stayed with me until I was all right again. She was so

gentle and so tender — I shall always love her
for that."

The sweet voice vibrated with feeling, and
Ruth's thoughts flew to the light in the attic
window, but, no — it could not be seen from
Miss Ainslie's. "What does Aunt Jane look
like?" she asked, after a pause.

"I haven't a picture, except one that was
taken a long time ago, but I'll get that." She
went upstairs and returned, presently, putting
an old-fashioned ambrotype into Ruth's hand.

The velvet-lined case enshrined Aunt Jane
in the bloom of her youth. It was a young
woman of twenty or twenty-five, seated in a
straight-backed chair, with her hands encased
in black lace mitts and folded in the lap of her
striped silk gown. The forehead was high,
protruding slightly, the eyes rather small, and
very dark, the nose straight, and the little chin
exceedingly firm and determined. There was
an expression of maidenly wistfulness somewhere, which Ruth could not definitely locate,
but there was no hint of it in the chin.

"Poor little Aunt Jane," said Ruth. "Life
never would be easy for her."

"No," returned Miss Ainslie, "but she
would not let anyone know."

Ruth strolled over to the window, thinking that she must be going, and Miss Ainslie still held the picture in her hand. "She had a lover, did n't she?" asked Ruth, idly.

"I — I — think so," answered the other, unwillingly. "You remember we quarrelled."

A young man stopped in the middle of the road, looked at Miss Ainslie's house, and then at the brown one across the hill. From her position in the window, Ruth saw him plainly. He hesitated a moment, then went toward the brown house. She noted that he was a stranger — there was no such topcoat in the village.

"Was his name Winfield?" she asked suddenly, then instantly hated herself for the question.

The ambrotype fell to the floor. Miss Ainslie stooped to pick it up and Ruth did not see her face. "Perhaps," she said, in a strange tone, "but I never have asked a lady the name of her friend."

Gentle as it was, Ruth felt the rebuke keenly. An apology was on her lips, but only her flushed cheeks betrayed any emotion. Miss Ainslie's face was pale, and there was unmistakable resentment in her eyes.

"I must go," Ruth said, after an awkward silence, and in an instant Miss Ainslie was herself again.

"No—you must n't go, deary. You have n't seen my garden yet. I have planted all the seeds and some of them are coming up. Is n't it beautiful to see things grow?"

"It is indeed," Ruth assented, forgetting the momentary awkwardness, "and I have lived for a long time where I have seen nothing grow but car tracks and high buildings. May I come again and see your garden?"

"I shall be so glad to have you," replied Miss Ainslie, with a quaint stateliness. "I have enjoyed your visit so much and I hope you will come again very soon."

"Thank you—I will."

Her hostess had opened the door for her, but Ruth stood in the hall, waiting, in obedience to some strange impulse. Then she stepped outside, but something held her back—something that lay unspoken between them. Those unfathomable eyes were fixed upon her, questioning, pleading, and searching her inmost soul.

Ruth looked at her, wondering, and striving to answer the mute appeal. Then Miss

Ainslie laid her hand upon her arm. "My dear," she asked, earnestly, "do you light the lamp in the attic window every night?"

"Yes, I do, Miss Ainslie," she answered, quickly.

The older woman caught her breath, as if in relief, and then the deep crimson flooded her face.

"Hepsey told me and Aunt Jane left a letter about it," Ruth continued, hastily, "and I am very glad to do it. It would be dreadful to have a ship wrecked, almost at our door."

"Yes," sighed Miss Ainslie, her colour receding, "I have often thought of 'those who go down to the sea in ships.' It is so terrible, and sometimes, when I hear the surf beating against the cliff, I—I am afraid."

Ruth climbed the hill, interested, happy, yet deeply disturbed. Miss Ainslie's beautiful, changing face seemed to follow her, and the exquisite scent of the lavender, which had filled the rooms, clung to her senses like a benediction.

Hepsey was right, and unquestionably Miss Ainslie had something to do with the light; but no deep meaning lay behind it—so much was certain. She had lived alone so long that

she had grown to have a great fear of shipwreck, possibly on account of her friend, the
"seafaring gentleman," and had asked Miss
Hathaway to put the light in the window—
that was all.

Ruth's reason was fully satisfied, but something else was not.   "I 'm not going to think
about it any more," she said to herself, resolutely, and thought she meant it.

She ate her dinner with the zest of hunger,
while Hepsey noiselessly served her.   "I
have been to Miss Ainslie's, Hepsey," she said
at length, not wishing to appear unsociable.

The maid's clouded visage cleared for an
instant.   "Did you find out about the lamp?"
she inquired, eagerly.

"No, I did n't, Hepsey; but I 'll tell you
what I think.   Miss Ainslie has read a great
deal and has lived alone so much that she has
become very much afraid of shipwreck.   You
know all of us have some one fear.   For instance, I am terribly afraid of green worms,
though a green worm has never harmed me.
I think she asked Miss Hathaway to put the
lamp in the window, and possibly told her of
something she had read which made her feel
that she should have done it before."

Hepsey's face took on its old, impenetrable calm.

"Don't you think so?" asked Miss Thorne, after a long pause.

"Yes 'm."

"It's all very reasonable, is n't it?"

"Yes 'm."

In spite of the seeming assent, she knew that Hepsey was not convinced; and afterward, when she came into the room with the attic lamp and a box of matches, the mystery returned to trouble Ruth again.

"If I don't take up tatting," she thought, as she went upstairs, "or find something else to do, I'll be a meddling old maid inside of six months."

IV

A Guest

AS the days went by, Ruth had the inevitable reaction. At first the country brought balm to her tired nerves, and she rested luxuriously, but she had not been at Miss Hathaway's a fortnight before she bitterly regretted the step she had taken.

Still there was no going back, for she had given her word, and must stay there until October. The months before her stretched out into a dreary waste. She thought of Miss Ainslie gratefully, as a redeeming feature, but she knew that it was impossible to spend all of her time in the house at the foot of the hill.

Half past six had seemed an unearthly hour for breakfast, and yet more than once Ruth had been downstairs at five o'clock, before Hepsey was stirring. There was no rest to be had anywhere, even after a long walk through the woods and fields. Inaction became irritation, and each day was filled with a thousand unbearable annoyances. She was fretful, moody, and restless, always wishing herself back in the office, yet knowing that she could not do good work, even if she were there.

She sat in her room one afternoon, frankly miserable, when Hepsey stalked in, unannounced, and gave her a card.

"Mr. Carl Winfield!" Ruth repeated aloud. "Some one to see me, Hepsey?" she asked, in astonishment.

"Yes 'm. He 's a-waitin' on the piazzer."

"Did n't you ask him to come in?"

"No 'm. Miss Hathaway, she don't want no strangers in her house."

"Go down immediately," commanded Ruth, sternly, "ask him into the parlour, and say that Miss Thorne will be down in a few moments."

"Yes 'm."

Hepsey shuffled downstairs with comfortable leisure, opened the door with aggravating slowness, then said, in a harsh tone that reached the upper rooms distinctly: "Miss Thorne, she says that you can come in and set in the parlour till she comes down."

"Thank you," responded a masculine voice, in quiet amusement; "Miss Thorne is kind—and generous."

Ruth's cheeks flushed hotly. "I don't know whether Miss Thorne will go down or not," she said to herself. "It's probably a book-agent."

She rocked pensively for a minute or two, wondering what would happen if she did not go down. There was no sound from the parlour save a subdued clearing of the throat. "He's getting ready to speak his piece," she thought, "and he might as well do it now as to wait for me."

Though she loathed Mr. Carl Winfield and his errand, whatever it might prove to be, she stopped before her mirror long enough to give a pat or two to her rebellious hair. On the way down she determined to be dignified, icy, and crushing.

A tall young fellow with a pleasant face rose to greet her as she entered the room. "Miss Thorne?" he inquired.

"Yes—please sit down. I am very sorry that my maid should have been so inhospitable." It was not what she had meant to say.

"Oh, that's all right," he replied, easily:

"I quite enjoyed it. I must ask your pardon for coming to you in this abrupt way, but Carlton gave me a letter to you, and I 've lost it." Carlton was the managing editor, and vague expectations of a summons to the office came into Ruth's mind.

"I 'm on *The Herald*," he went on; "that is, I was, until my eyes gave out, and then they did n't want me any more. Newspapers can't use anybody out of repair," he added, grimly.

"I know," Ruth answered, nodding.

"Of course the office is n't a sanitarium, though they need that kind of an annex; nor yet a literary kindergarten, which I 've known it to be taken for, but—well, I won't tell you my troubles. The oculist said I must go to the country for six months, stay outdoors, and neither read nor write. I went to see Carlton, and he promised me a berth in the Fall—they 're going to have a morning edition, too, you know."

Miss Thorne did not know, but she was much interested.

"Carlton advised me to come up here," resumed Winfield. "He said you were here, and that you were going back in the Fall. I 'm sorry I 've lost his letter."

"What was in it?" inquired Ruth, with a touch of sarcasm.   "You read it, did n't you?"

"Of course I read it—that is, I tried to. The thing looked like a prescription, but, as nearly as I could make it out, it was principally a description of the desolation in the office since you left it.   At the end there was a line or two commending me to your tender mercies, and here I am."

"Commending yourself."

"Now what in the dickens have I done?" thought Winfield.   "That 's it exactly, Miss Thorne.   I 've lost my reference, and I 'm doing my best to create a good impression without it.   I thought that as long as we were going to be on the same paper, and were both exiles——"

He paused, and she finished the sentence for him: "that you 'd come to see me.   How long have you been in town?"

"'In town' is good," he said.   "I arrived in this desolate, God-forsaken spot just ten days ago.   Until now I 've hunted and fished every day, but I did n't get anything but a cold.   It was very good, of its kind—I could n't speak above a whisper for three days."

She had already recognised him as the young man she saw standing in the road the day she went to Miss Ainslie's, and mentally asked his pardon for thinking he was a book-agent. He might become a pleasant acquaintance, for he was tall, clean shaven, and well built. His hands were white and shapely and he was well groomed, though not in the least foppish. The troublesome eyes were dark brown, sheltered by a pair of tinted glasses. His face was very expressive, responding readily to every change of mood.

They talked "shop" for a time, discovering many mutual friends, and Ruth liked him. He spoke easily, though hurriedly, and appeared to be somewhat cynical, but she rightly attributed it to restlessness like her own.

"What are you going to do on *The Tribune?*" she asked.

"Anything," he answered, with an indefinable shrug. "'Theirs not to reason why, theirs but to do and die.' What are you going to do?"

"The same," replied Ruth. "'Society,' 'Mother's Corner,' 'Under the Evening Lamp,' and 'In the Kitchen with Aunt Jenny.'"

He laughed infectiously. "I wish Carlton would hear you say that."

"I don't," returned Ruth, colouring faintly.

"Why; are you afraid of him?"

"Certainly I am. If he speaks to me, I'm instantly stiff with terror."

"Oh, he isn't so bad," said Winfield, re-assuringly. "He's naturally abrupt, that's all; and I'll venture he doesn't suspect that he has any influence over you. I'd never fancy that you were afraid of anybody or anything on earth."

"I'm not afraid of anything else," she answered, "except burglars and green worms."

"Carlton would enjoy the classification— really, Miss Thorne, somebody should tell him, don't you think? So much innocent pleasure doesn't often come into the day of a busy man."

For a moment Ruth was angry, and then, all at once, she knew Winfield as if he had always been her friend. Conventionality, years, and the veneer of society were lightly laid upon one who would always be a boy. Some men are old at twenty, but Winfield would be young at seventy.

"You can tell him if you want to," Ruth

rejoined, calmly. "He'll be so pleased that he'll double your salary on the spot."

"And you?" he asked, his eyes twinkling with fun.

"I'll be pensioned, of course."

"You're all right," he returned, "but I guess I won't tell him. Riches lead to temptation, and if I'm going to be on *The Tribune* I'd hate to have you pensioned."

Hepsey appeared to have a great deal of employment in the dining-room, and was very quiet about it, with long pauses between her leisurely movements. Winfield did not seem to notice it, but it jarred upon Ruth, and she was relieved when he said he must go.

"You'll come again, won't you?" she asked.

"I will, indeed."

She stood at the window, unconsciously watching him as he went down the hill with a long, free stride. She liked the strength in his broad shoulders, his well modulated voice, and his clear, honest eyes; but after all he was nothing but a boy.

"Miss Thorne," said Hepsey, at her elbow, "is that your beau?" It was not impertinence, but sheer friendly interest which could not be mistaken for anything else.

"No," she answered; "of course not."

"He's real nice-lookin', ain't he?"

"Yes."

"Have you got your eye on anybody else?"

"No."

"Then, Miss Thorne, I don't know 's you could do better."

"Perhaps not." She was thinking, and spoke mechanically. From where she stood she could still see him walking rapidly down the hill.

"Ain't you never seen him before?"

Miss Thorne turned. "Hepsey," she said, coldly, "please go into the kitchen and attend to your work. And the next time I have company, please stay in the kitchen — not in the dining-room."

"Yes 'm," replied Hepsey, meekly, hastening to obey.

She was not subtle, but she understood that in some way she had offended Miss Thorne, and racked her brain vainly. She had said nothing that she would not have said to Miss Hathaway, and had intended nothing but friendliness. As for her being in the dining-room—why, very often, when Miss Hathaway had company, she was called in to give her version of some bit of village gossip. Miss Hathaway scolded her when she was displeased, but never before had any one spoken to Hepsey in a measured, icy tone that was at once lady-like and commanding. Tears came into her eyes, for she was sensitive, after all.

A step sounded overhead, and Hepsey regained her self-possession. She had heard nearly all of the conversation and could have told Miss Thorne a great deal about the young man. For instance, he had not said that he was boarding at Joe's, across the road from Miss Ainslie's, and that he intended to stay all Summer. She could have told her of an uncertain temper, peculiar tastes, and of a silver shaving-cup which Joe had promised her a glimpse of before the visitor went back to the city; but she decided to let Miss Thorne go on in her blind ignorance.

Ruth, meanwhile, was meditating, with an aggravated restlessness. The momentary glimpse of the outer world had stung her into a sense of her isolation, which she realised even more keenly than before. It was because of this, she told herself, that she hoped Winfield liked her, for it was not her wont to care about such trifles. He thought of her, idly, as a nice girl, who was rather pretty when she was interested in anything; but, with a woman's insight, influenced insensibly by Hepsey's comment, Ruth scented possibilities.

She wanted him to like her, to stay in that miserable village as long as she did, and keep her mind from stagnation—her thought went no farther than that. In October, when they went back, she would thank Carlton, prettily, for sending her a friend—provided they did not quarrel. She could see long days of intimate companionship, of that exalted kind which is possible only when man and woman meet on a high plane. "We're both too old for nonsense," she thought; and then a sudden fear struck her,—that Winfield might be several years younger than she was.

Immediately she despised herself. "I don't care if he is," she thought, with her cheeks crimson; "it's nothing to me. He's a nice boy, and I want to be amused."

She went to her dresser, took out the large top drawer, and dumped its contents on the bed. It was a desperate measure, for Ruth hated to put things in order. The newspaper which had lain in the bottom of it had fallen out also, and she shook it so violently that she tore it.

Then ribbons, handkerchiefs, stocks, gloves, and collars were unceremoniously hustled back into the drawer, for Miss Thorne was at odds with herself and the world. She was angry with Hepsey, she hated Winfield, and despised herself. She picked up a scrap of paper whi h lay on a glove, and caught a glimpse of unfamiliar penmanship.

It was apparently the end of a letter, and the rest of it was gone. "At Gibraltar for some time," she read, "keeping a shop, but will probably be found now in some small town on the coast of Italy. Very truly yours." The signature had been torn off.

"Why, that is n't mine," she thought. "It must be something of Aunt Jane's." Another bit of paper lay near it, and, unthinkingly, she read a letter which was not meant for her.

"I thank you from my heart," it began, "for understanding me. I could not put it into words, but I believe you know. Perhaps you think it is useless—that it is too late; but if it was, I would know. You have been very kind, and I thank you."

There was neither date, address, nor signature. The message stood alone, as absolutely as some far-off star whose light could not be seen from the earth. Some one understood it — two understood it — the writer and Aunt Jane.

Ruth put it back, under the paper, with the scrap of the other letter, and closed the drawer with a bang. "I hope," she said to herself, "that while I stay here I'll be mercifully preserved from finding things that are none of my business." Then, as in a lightning flash, for an instant she saw clearly.

Fate plays us many tricks and assumes strange forms, but Ruth knew that some day, on that New England hill, she would come face to face with a destiny that had been ordained from the beginning. Something waited for her there—some great change. She trembled at the thought, but was not afraid.

V

The Rumours of the Valley

"MISS THORNE," said Hepsey, from the doorway of Ruth's room, "that feller's here again." There was an unconscious emphasis on the last word, and Ruth herself was somewhat surprised, for she had not expected another call so soon.

"He's a-settin' in the parlour," continued Hepsey, "when he ain't a-walkin' around it and wearin' out the carpet. I did n't come up when he first come, on account of my pie crust bein' all ready to put in the oven."

"How long has he been here?" asked Ruth, dabbing a bit of powder on her nose and selecting a fresh collar.

"Oh, p'raps half an hour."

"That is n't right, Hepsey; when any one comes you must tell me immediately. Never mind the pie crust next time." Ruth endeavoured to speak kindly, but she was irritated at the necessity of making another apology.

When she went down, Winfield dismissed her excuses with a comprehensive wave of the hand. "I always have to wait when I go to call on a girl," he said; "it's one of the most charming vagaries of the ever-feminine. I used to think that perhaps I was n't popular, but every fellow I know has the same experience."

"I'm an exception," explained Ruth; "I never keep any one waiting. Of my own volition, that is," she added, hastily, feeling his unspoken comment.

"I came up this afternoon to ask a favour of you," he began. "Won't you go for a walk with me? It's wrong to stay indoors on a day like this."

"Wait till I get my hat," said Ruth, rising.

"Fifteen minutes is the limit," he called to her, as she went upstairs.

She was back again almost immediately, and Hepsey watched them in wide-mouthed astonishment as they went down hill together, for it was not in her code of manners that "walking out" should begin so soon. When they approached Miss Ainslie's he pointed out the brown house across from it, on the other side of the hill.

"Yonder palatial mansion is my present lodging," he volunteered, "and I am a helpless fly in the web of the 'Widder' Pendleton."

"Pendleton," repeated Ruth; "why, that's Joe's name."

"It is," returned Winfield, concisely. "He sits opposite me at the table, and wonders at my use of a fork. It is considered merely a spear for bread and meat at the 'Widder's.' I am observed closely at all times, and in some respects Joe admires me enough to attempt imitation, which, as you know, is the highest form of flattery. For instance, this morning he wore not only a collar and tie, but a scarf pin. It was a string tie, and I've never before seen a pin worn in one, but it's interesting."

"It must be."

"He has a sweetheart," Winfield went on, "and I expect she'll be dazzled."

"My Hepsey is his lady love," Ruth explained.

"What? The haughty damsel who would n't let me in? Do tell!"

"You're imitating now," laughed Ruth, "but I should n't call it flattery."

"No? It all depends on the way you look at it. The point of view is everything in this world. Yours is naturally lofty because you live on a hill."

As they passed Miss Ainslie's house, Ruth had a glimpse of a lavender gown, flitting among the flower beds, then, in a moment, the hedge screened her.

"I've heard all the village gossip," he said. "The secluded person across the way is half crazy."

"She is not," retorted Ruth, indignantly. "She's the dearest, sweetest woman in the whole world."

Winfield liked her spirit and her loyalty, but he merely said: "Why vilify the phonograph? I am but the humble instrument of repetition."

"You should n't repeat such things!"

"Excuse me—I'll never do it again. I forgot, for the moment, that you were 'a lady detective.'"

The colour flamed in her cheeks. "What do you mean?" she demanded.

"Pray calm yourself, Miss Thorne—there is really no immediate danger. There is plenty of time to launch the life-boat before the ship turns over."

His teasing manner made her realise that she was making herself ridiculous. "I won't be cross," she said, pleasantly. "Tell me all the village gossip."

"'Consistency, thou art a jewel.'"

"Because of scarcity," she commented, as they turned into a path which led to the woods.

"Is it possible that a dweller on the heights should care for the rumours of the valley?"

"Not only possible, but probable."

"Very well, Miss Thorne. You are said to be a peculiar woman and I cannot deny the report. I have no authority to deny it," he added, as Ruth flashed a meaning glance at him. "You have burned oil until after ten o'clock at night, have gone spooking around the house at all hours, and have once spent a whole day in the attic."

Ruth was looking straight ahead, with her chin held high and a faint flush on her face. Winfield looked at her pure, proud profile, and wondered if he dared. The poise of her head was distinctly discouraging, but he was naturally fond of adventure, so he cleared his throat and took a deep plunge.

"You have large feet and wear men's shoes."

For a moment, there was a chilly silence. Ruth did not look at him, but she bit her lip and then laughed, unwillingly. "It's all true," she said, "I plead guilty."

"You see, I know all about you," he went on. "You knit your brows in deep thought, do not hear when you are spoken to, even in a loud voice, and your mail consists almost entirely of bulky envelopes, of a legal nature, such as came to the 'Widder' Pendleton from the insurance people."

"Returned manuscripts," she interjected.

"Possibly—far be it from me to say they're not. Why, I've had 'em myself."

"You don't mean it!" she exclaimed, ironically.

"You seek out, as if by instinct, the only crazy person in the village, and come home greatly perturbed. You ask queer questions of your humble serving-maid, assume a skirt which is shorter than the approved model, speaking from the village standpoint, and unhesitatingly appear on the public streets. You go to the attic at night and search the inmost recesses of many old trunks."

"Yes," sighed Ruth, "I've done all that."

"At breakfast you refuse pie, and complain

because the coffee is boiled. Did anybody ever hear of coffee that was n't boiled? Is it eaten raw in the city? You call supper 'dinner,' and have been known to seek nourishment at nine o'clock at night, when all respectable people are sound asleep. In your trunk, you have vainly attempted to conceal a large metal object, the use of which is unknown."

"Oh, my hapless chafing-dish!" groaned Ruth.

"Chafing-dish?" repeated Winfield, brightening visibly. "And I eating sole leather and fried potatoes? From this hour I am your slave—you can't lose me now!"

"Go on," she commanded.

"I can't — the flow of my eloquence is stopped by rapturous anticipation. Suffice it to say that the people of this enterprising city are well up in the ways of the wicked world, for the storekeeper takes *The New York Weekly* and the 'Widder' Pendleton subscribes for *The Fireside Companion*. The back numbers, which are not worn out, are the circulating library of the village. It 's no use, Miss Thorne—you might stand on your hilltop and proclaim your innocence until you were hoarse, and it would be utterly without effect. Your status is definitely settled."

"How about Aunt Jane?" she inquired. "Does my relationship count for naught?"

"Now you are rapidly approaching the centre of things," replied the young man. "Miss Hathaway is one woman in a thousand, though somewhat eccentric. She is the venerated pillar of the community and a constant attendant at church, which it seems you are not. Also, if you are really her niece, where is the family resemblance? Why has she never spoken of you? Why have you never been here before? Why are her letters to you sealed with red wax, bought especially for the purpose? Why does she go away before you come? Lady Gwendolen Hetherington." he demanded, with melodramatic fervour, "answer me these things if you can!"

"I'm tired," she complained.

"Delicate compliment," observed Winfield, apparently to himself. "Here's a log across our path, Miss Thorne; let's sit down."

The budded maples arched over the narrow path, and a wild canary, singing in the sun, hopped from bough to bough. A robin's cheery chirp came from another tree, and the clear notes of a thrush, with a mottled breast, were answered by another in the gold-green aisles beyond.

"Oh," he said, under his breath, "isn't this great!"

The exquisite peace of the forest was like that of another sphere. "Yes," she answered, softly, "it is beautiful."

"You're evading the original subject," he suggested, a little later.

"I haven't had a chance to talk," she explained. "You've done a monologue ever since we left the house, and I listened, as becomes inferior and subordinate woman. I have never seen my venerated kinswoman, and I don't see how she happened to think of me. Nevertheless, when she wrote, asking me to take charge of her house while she went to Europe, I gladly consented, sight unseen. When I came, she was gone. I do not deny the short skirt and heavy shoes, the criticism of boiled coffee, nor the disdain of breakfast pie. As far as I know, Aunt Jane is my only living relative."

"That's good," he said, cheerfully; "I'm shy even of an aunt. Why shouldn't the orphans console one another?"

"They should," admitted Ruth; "and you are doing your share nobly."

"Permit me to return the compliment. Honestly, Miss Thorne," he continued, seriously, "you have no idea how much I appreciate your being here. When I first realised what it meant to be deprived of books and papers for six months at a stretch, it seemed as if I should go mad. Still, I suppose six months is n't as bad as forever, and I was given a c oice. I don't want to bore you, but if you will let me come occasionally, I shall be very glad. I'm going to try to be patient, too, if you'll help me—patience is n't my long suit."

"Indeed I will help you," answered Ruth, impulsively; "I know how hard it must be."

"I'm not begging for your sympathy, though I assure you it is welcome." He polished the tinted glasses with a bit of chamois, and his eyes filled with the mist of weakness before he put them on again. "So you've never seen your aunt," he said.

"No—that pleasure is still in store for me."

"They say down at the 'Widder's' that she's a woman with a romance."

"Tell me about it!" exclaimed Ruth, eagerly.

"Little girls must n't ask questions," he remarked, patronisingly, and in his most irritating manner. "Besides, I don't know. If the 'Widder' knows, she won't tell, so it 's fair to suppose she does n't. Your relation does queer things in the attic, and every Spring, she has an annual weep. I suppose it's the house cleaning, for the rest of the year she 's dry-eyed and calm."

"I weep very frequently," commented Ruth.

"'Tears, idle tears—I wonder what they mean.'"

"They don't mean much, in the case of a woman."

"I 've never seen many of 'em," returned Winfield, "and I don't want to. Even stage tears go against the grain with me. I know that the lady who sobs behind the footlights is well paid for it, but all the same, it gives me the creeps."

"It 's nothing serious—really it is n't," she explained. "It 's merely a safety valve. If women could n't cry, they 'd explode."

"I always supposed tears were signs of sorrow," he said.

"Far from it," laughed Ruth. "When I

get very angry, I cry, and then I get angrier because I 'm crying and cry harder."

"That opens up a fearful possibility. What would happen if you kept getting angrier because you were crying and crying harder because you got angrier?"

"I have no idea," she answered, with her dark eyes fixed upon him, "but it 's a promising field for investigation."

"I don't want to see the experiment."

"Don't worry," said Ruth, laconically, "you won't."

There was a long silence, and Winfield began to draw designs on the bare earth with a twig. "Tell me about the lady who is considered crazy," he suggested.

Ruth briefly described Miss Ainslie, dwelling lovingly upon her beauty and charm. He listened indifferently at first, but when she told him of the rugs, the real lace which edged the curtains, and the Cloisonné vase, he became much interested.

"Take me to see her some day, won't you," he asked, carelessly.

Ruth's eyes met his squarely. "'T is n't a 'story,'" she said, resentfully, forgetting her own temptation.

The dull colour flooded his face. "You forget, Miss Thorne, that I am forbidden to read or write."

"For six months only," answered Ruth, sternly, "and there's always a place for a good Sunday special."

He changed the subject, but there were frequent awkward pauses and the spontaniety was gone. She rose, adjusting her belt in the back, and announced that it was time for her to go home.

On their way up the hill, she tried to be gracious enough to atone for her rudeness, but, though he was politeness itself, there was a difference, and she felt as if she had lost something. Distance lay between them—a cold, immeasurable distance, yet she knew that she had done right.

He opened the gate for her, then turned to go. "Won't you come in?" she asked, conventionally.

"No, thank you—some other time, if I may. I've had a charming afternoon." He smiled pleasantly, and was off down the hill.

When she remembered that it was a Winfield who had married Abigail Weatherby, she dismissed the matter as mere coincidence, and determined, at all costs, to shield Miss Ainslie. The vision of that gracious lady came to her, bringing with it a certain uplift of soul. Instantly, she was placed far above the petty concerns of earth, like one who walks upon the heights, untroubled, while restless surges thunder at his feet.

VI

The Garden

MISS THORNE wrote an apology to Winfield, and then tore it up, thereby gaining comparative peace of mind, for, with
some natures, expression is the main thing,
and direction is but secondary. She was not
surprised because he did not come; on the
contrary, she had rather expected to be left to
her own devices for a time, but one afternoon
she dressed with unusual care and sat in state
in the parlour, vaguely expectant. If he intended to be friendly, it was certainly time for
him to come again.

Hepsey, passing through the hall, noted the
crisp white ribbon at her throat and the bow
in her hair. "Are you expectin' company,
Miss Thorne?" she asked, innocently.

"I am expecting no one," answered Ruth,
frigidly, "I am going out."

Feeling obliged to make her word good,

she took the path which led to Miss Ainslie's.
As she entered the gate, she had a glimpse of
Winfield, sitting by the front window of Mrs.
Pendleton's brown house, in such a dejected
attitude that she pitied him.   She considered
the virtuous emotion very praiseworthy, even
though it was not deep enough for her to be-
stow a cheery nod upon the gloomy person
across the way.

Miss Ainslie was unaffectedly glad to see
her, and Ruth sank into an easy chair with
something like content.   The atmosphere of
the place was insensibly soothing and she instantly felt a subtle change.   Miss Ainslie, as
always, wore a lavender gown, with real lace
at the throat and wrists.   Her white hair was
waved softly and on the third finger of her left
hand was a ring of Roman gold, set with an
amethyst and two large pearls.

There was a beautiful serenity about her,
evident in every line of her face and figure.
Time had dealt gently with her, and except
on her queenly head had left no trace of his
passing.   The delicate scent of the lavender
floated from her gown and her laces, almost as
if it were a part of her, and brought visions of
an old-time garden, whose gentle mistress was

ever tranquil and content. As she sat there,
smiling, she might have been Peace grown
old.

"Miss Ainslie," said Ruth, suddenly, "have
you ever had any trouble?"

A shadow crossed her face, and then she
answered, patiently, "Why, yes—I 've had
my share."

"I don't mean to be personal," Ruth explained, "I was just thinking."

"I understand," said the other, gently.
Then, after a little, she spoke again:

"We all have trouble, deary — it 's part of
life; but I believe that we all share equally in
the joy of the world. Allowing for tempera-
ment, I mean. Sorrows that would crush
some are lightly borne by others, and some
have the gift of finding great happiness in
little things.

"Then, too, we never have any more than
we can bear — nothing that has not been
borne before, and bravely at that. There
is n't a new sorrow in the world — they 're
all old ones — but we can all find new happiness if we look in the right way."

The voice had a full music, instinct with
tenderness, and gradually Ruth's troubled

spirit was eased. "I don't know what's the matter with me," she said, meditatively, "for I'm not morbid, and I don't have the blues very often, but almost ever since I've been at Aunt Jane's I've been restless and disturbed. I know there's no reason for it, but I can't help it."

"Don't you think that it's because you have nothing to do? You've always been so busy, and you aren't used to idleness."

"Perhaps so. I miss my work, but at the same time, I haven't sense enough to do it."

"Poor child, you're tired—too tired to rest."

"Yes, I am tired," answered Ruth, the tears of nervous weakness coming into her eyes.

"Come out into the garden."

Miss Ainslie drew a fleecy shawl over her shoulders and led her guest outdoors. Though she kept pace with the world in many other ways, it was an old-fashioned garden, with a sun-dial and an arbour, and little paths, nicely kept, that led to the flower beds and circled around them. There were no flowers as yet, except in a bed of wild violets under a bay window, but tiny sprigs of green were everywhere eloquent with promise, and the lilacs were budded.

"That's a snowball bush over there," said Miss Ainslie, "and all that corner of the garden will be full of roses in June. They're old-fashioned roses, that I expect you would n't care for — blush and cinnamon and sweet briar — but I love them all. That long row is half peonies and half bleeding-hearts, and I have a bed of columbines under a window on the other side of the house. The mignonette and forget-me-nots have a place to themselves, for I think they belong together — sweetness and memory.

"There's going to be lady-slippers over there," Miss Ainslie went on, "and sweet william. The porch is always covered with morning-glories — I think they're beautiful — and in that large bed I 've planted poppies, snap-dragon, and marigolds. This round one is full of larkspur and bachelor's buttons. I have phlox and petunias, too — did you ever see a petunia seed?"

Ruth shook her head.

"It's the tiniest thing, smaller than a grain of sand. When I plant them, I always wonder how those great, feathery petunias are coming out of those little, baby seeds, but they come. Over there are things that won't blossom till late — asters, tiger-lilies and prince's feather. It's going to be a beautiful garden, deary. Down by the gate are my sweet herbs and simples — marjoram, sweet thyme, rosemary, and lavender. I love the lavender, don't you?"

"Yes, I do," replied Ruth, "but I've never seen it growing."

"It's a little bush, with lavender flowers that yield honey, and it's all sweet — flowers, leaves, and all. I expect you'll laugh at me, but I've planted sunflowers and four-o'clocks and foxglove."

"I won't laugh — I think it's lovely. What do you like best, Miss Ainslie?"

"I love them all," she said, with a smile on her lips and her deep, unfathomable eyes fixed upon Ruth, "but I think the lavender comes first. It's so sweet, and then it has associations ——"

She paused, in confusion, and Ruth went on, quickly: "I think they all have associations, and that's why we love them. I can't bear red geraniums because a cross old woman I knew when I was a child had her yard full of them, and I shall always love the lavender," she added, softly, "because it makes me think of you."

Miss Ainslie's cheeks flushed and her eyes shone. "Now we'll go into the house," she said, "and we'll have tea."

"I should n't stay any longer," murmured Ruth, following her, "I've been here so long now."

"'T is n't long," contradicted Miss Ainslie, sweetly, "it's been only a very few minutes."

Every moment, the house and its owner took on new beauty and charm. Miss Ainslie spread a napkin of finest damask upon the little mahogany tea table, then brought in a silver teapot of quaint design, and two cups of Japanese china, dainty to the point of fragility.

"Why, Miss Ainslie," exclaimed Ruth, in surprise, "where did you get Royal Kaga?"

Miss Ainslie was bending over the table, and the white hand that held the teapot trembled a little. "They were a present from —a friend," she answered, in a low voice.

"They're beautiful," said Ruth, hurriedly. She had been to many an elaborate affair, which was down on the social calendar as a "tea," sometimes as reporter and often as guest, but she had found no hostess like Miss Ainslie, no china so exquisitely fine, nor any

tea like the clear, fragrant amber which was
poured into her cup.

"It came from China," said Miss Ainslie,
feeling the unspoken question. "I had a
whole chest of it, but it 's almost all gone."

Ruth was turning her cup and consulting
the oracle. "Here 's two people, a man and
a woman, from a great distance, and, yes,
here 's money, too. What is there in yours?"

"Nothing, deary, and besides, it does n't
come true."

When Ruth finally aroused herself to go
home, the old restlessness, for the moment,
was gone. "There 's a charm about you,"
she said, "for I feel as if I could sleep a whole
week and never wake at all."

"It 's the tea," smiled Miss Ainslie, "for
I 'm a very commonplace body."

"You, commonplace?" repeated Ruth;
"why, there 's nobody like you!"

They stood at the door a few moments,
talking aimlessly, but Ruth was watching Miss
Ainslie's face, as the sunset light lay caressingly upon it. "I 've had a lovely time,"
she said, taking another step toward the
gate.

"So have I — you 'll come again, won't

you ?" The sweet voice was pleading now, and Ruth answered it in her inmost soul. Impulsively, she came back, threw her arms around Miss Ainslie's neck, and kissed her. "I love you," she said, "don't you know I do ?"

The quick tears filled Miss Ainslie's eyes and she smiled through the mist. "Thank you, deary," she whispered, "it's a long time since any one has kissed me — a long time!"

Ruth turned back at the gate, to wave her hand, and even at that distance, saw that Miss Ainslie was very pale.

Winfield was waiting for her, just outside the hedge, but his presence jarred upon her strangely, and her salutation was not cordial.

"Is the lady a friend of yours?" he inquired, indifferently.

"She is," returned Ruth; "I don't go to see my enemies—do you?"

"I don't know whether I do or not," he said, looking at her significantly.

Her colour rose, but she replied, sharply: "For the sake of peace, let us assume that you do not."

"Miss Thorne," he began, as they climbed

the hill, "I don't see why you don't apply something cooling to your feverish temper. You have to live with yourself all the time, you know, and, occasionally, it must be very difficult. A rag, now, wet in cold water, and tied around your neck—have you ever tried that? It 's said to be very good."

"I have one on now," she answered, with apparent seriousness, "only you can't see it under my ribbon. It 's getting dry and I think I 'd better hurry home to wet it again, don't you?"

Winfield laughed joyously. "You 'll do," he said.

Before they were half up the hill, they were on good terms again. "I don't want to go home, do you?" he asked.

"Home? I have no home—I 'm only a poor working girl."

"Oh, what would this be with music! I can see it now! Ladies and gentlemen, with your kind permission, I will endeavour to give you a little song of my own composition, entitled: 'Why Has the Working Girl No Home!'"

"You have n't my permission, and you 're a wretch."

"I am," he admitted, cheerfully, "moreover, I 'm a worm in the dust."

"I don't like worms."

"Then you 'll have to learn."

Ruth resented his calm assumption of mastery. "You 're dreadfully young," she said; "do you think you 'll ever grow up?"

"Huh!" returned Winfield, boyishly, "I 'm most thirty."

"Really? I should n't have thought you were of age."

"Here 's a side path, Miss Thorne," he said, abruptly, "that seems to go down into the woods. Shall we explore? It won't be dark for an hour yet."

They descended with some difficulty, since the way was not clear, and came into the woods at a point not far from the log across the path. "We must n't sit there any more," he observed, "or we 'll fight. That 's where we were the other day, when you attempted to assassinate me."

"I did n't!" exclaimed Ruth indignantly.

"That rag does seem to be pretty dry," he said, apparently to himself. "Perhaps, when we get to the sad sea, we can wet it, and so insure comparative calm."

She laughed, reluctantly. The path led around the hill and down from the highlands to a narrow ledge of beach that lay under the cliff. "Do you want to drown me?" she asked. "It looks very much as if you intended to, for this ledge is covered at high tide."

"You wrong me, Miss Thorne; I have never drowned anything."

His answer was lost upon her, for she stood on the beach, under the cliff, looking at the water. The shimmering turquoise blue was slowly changing to grey, and a single sea gull circled overhead.

He made two or three observations, to which Ruth paid no attention. "My Lady Disdain," he said, with assumed anxiety, "don't you think we'd better go on? I don't know what time the tide comes in, and I never could look your aunt in the face if I had drowned her only relative."

"Very well," she replied carelessly, "let's go around the other way."

They followed the beach until they came to the other side of the hill, but found no path leading back to civilisation, though the ascent could easily be made.

"People have been here before," he said;
"here are some initials cut into this stone.
What are they? I can't see."

Ruth stooped to look at the granite boulder
he indicated. "J. H.," she answered, "and
J. B."

"It's incomplete," he objected; "there
should be a heart with an arrow run through it."

"You can fix it to suit yourself," Ruth returned, coolly, "I don't think anybody will
mind." She did not hear his reply, for it
suddenly dawned upon her that "J. H."
meant Jane Hathaway.

They stood there in the twilight for some
little time, watching the changing colours on
the horizon, and then there was a faint glow
on the water from the cliff above. Ruth went
out far enough to see that Hepsey had placed
the lamp in the attic window.

"It's time to go," she said, "inasmuch as
we have to go back the way we came."

They crossed to the other side and went
back through the woods. It was dusk, and
they walked rapidly until they came to the log
across the path.

"So your friend isn't crazy," he said tentatively, as he tried to assist her over it.

"That depends," she replied, drawing away from him; "you're indefinite."

"Forgot to wet the rag, did n't we?" he asked. "I will gladly assume the implication, however, if I may be your friend."

"Kind, I 'm sure," she answered, with distant politeness.

The path widened, and he walked by her side. "Have you noticed, Miss Thorne, that we have trouble every time we approach that seemingly innocent barrier? I think it would be better to keep away from it, don't you?"

"Perhaps."

"What initials were those on the boulder? J. H. and —— "

"J. B."

"I thought so. 'J. B.' must have had a lot of spare time at his disposal, for his initials are cut into the 'Widder' Pendleton's gate post on the inner side, and into an apple tree in the back yard."

"How interesting!"

"Did you know Joe and Hepsey were going out to-night?"

"No, I did n't — they 're not my intimate friends."

"I don't see how Joe expects to marry on
the income derived from the village chariot."

"Have they got that far?"

"I don't know," replied Winfield, with the
air of one imparting a confidence. "You see,
though I have been in this peaceful village for
some little time, I have not yet arrived at the
fine distinction between 'walking out,' 'settin'
up,' and 'stiddy comp'ny.' I should infer
that 'walking out' came first, for 'settin' up'
must take a great deal more courage, but even
I, with my vast intellect, cannot at present
understand 'stiddy comp'ny.'"

"Joe takes her out every Sunday in the carriage," volunteered Ruth, when the silence
became awkward.

"In the what?"

"Carriage — have n't you ridden in it?"

"I have ridden in them, but not in it. I
walked to the 'Widder's,' but if it is the conveyance used by travellers, they are both
'walking out' and 'settin' up.'"

They paused at the gate. "Thank you for
a pleasant afternoon," said Winfield. "I don't
have many of them."

"You 're welcome," returned Ruth, conveying the impression of great distance.

Winfield sighed, then made a last desperate attempt. "Miss Thorne," he said, pleadingly, "please don't be unkind to me. You have my reason in your hands. I can see myself now, sitting on the floor, at one end of the danger-ous ward. They 'll smear my fingers with molasses and give me half a dozen feathers to play with. You 'll come to visit the asylum, sometime, when you 're looking for a special, and at first, you won't recognise me. Then I 'll say: 'Woman, behold your work,' and you 'll be miserable all the rest of your life."

She laughed heartily at the distressing pic-ture, and the plaintive tone of his voice pierced her armour. "What 's the matter with you?" she asked.

"I don't know — I suppose it 's my eyes. I 'm horribly restless and discontented, and it is n't my way."

Then Ruth remembered her own restless weeks, which seemed so long ago, and her heart stirred with womanly sympathy. "I know," she said, in a different tone, "I 've felt the same way myself, almost ever since I 've been here, until this very afternoon. You 're tired and nervous, and you have n't anything to do, but you 'll get over it."

"I hope you 're right. I 've been getting Joe to read the papers to me, at a quarter a sitting, but his pronunciation is so unfamiliar that it 's hard to get the drift, and the whole thing exasperated me so that I had to give it up."

"Let me read the papers to you," she said, impulsively, "I have n't seen one for a month."

There was a long silence. "I don't want to impose upon you," he answered — "no, you must n't do it."

Ruth saw a stubborn pride that shrank from the slightest dependence, a self-reliance that would not falter, but would steadfastly hold aloof, and she knew that in one thing at least, they were kindred.

"Let me," she cried, eagerly; "I 'll give you my eyes for a little while!"

Winfield caught her hand and held it for a moment, fully understanding. Ruth's eyes looked up into his — deep, dark, dangerously appealing, and alight with generous desire.

His fingers unclasped slowly. "Yes, I will," he said, strangely moved. "It 's a beautiful gift — in more ways than one. You are very kind — thank you — good night!"

VII

The Man Who Hesitates

"'TIS N'T fair," said Winfield to himself, miserably, "no sir, 't is n't fair!"

He sat on the narrow piazza which belonged to Mrs. Pendleton's brown house, and took stern account of his inner self. The morning paper lay beside him, unopened, though his fingers itched to tear the wrapper, and his hat was pulled far down over his eyes, to shade them from the sun.

"If I go up there I'm going to fall in love with her, and I know it!"

That moment of revelation the night before, when soul stood face to face with soul, had troubled him strangely. He knew himself for a sentimentalist where women were concerned, but until they stood at the gate together, he had thought himself safe. Like many another man, on the sunny side of thirty, he had his ideal

woman safely enshrined in his inner consciousness.

She was a pretty little thing, this dream
maiden—a blonde, with deep blue eyes, a
rosy complexion, and a mouth like Cupid's
bow.   Mentally, she was of the clinging sort,
for Winfield did not know that in this he was
out of fashion.   She had a dainty, bird-like
air about her and a high, sweet voice—a most
adorable little woman, truly, for a man to
dream of when business was not too
pressing.

In almost every possible way, Miss Thorne
was different.   She was dark, and nearly as
tall as he was; dignified, self-possessed, and
calm, except for flashes of temper and that
one impulsive moment.   He had liked her,
found her interesting in a tantalising sort of
way, and looked upon her as an oasis in a
social desert, but that was all.

Of course, he might leave the village, but
he made a wry face upon discovering, through
laboured analysis, that he did n't want to go
away.   It was really a charming spot—hunt-
ing and fishing to be had for the asking, fine
accommodations at Mrs. Pendleton's, beautiful scenery, bracing air—in every way it was

just what he needed.   Should he let himself
be frightened out of it by a newspaper woman
who lived at the top of the hill?   Hardly!

None the less, he realised that a man might
firmly believe in Affinity, and, through a
chain of unfortunate circumstances, become
the victim of Propinquity.   He had known of
such instances and was now face to face with
the dilemma.

Then his face flooded with dull colour.
"Darn it," he said to himself, savagely,
"what an unmitigated cad I am!   All this is
on the assumption that she's likely to fall on
my neck at any minute!   Lord!"

Yet there was a certain comfort in the
knowledge that he was safe, even if he should
fall in love with Miss Thorne.   That disdainful
young woman would save him from himself,
undoubtedly, when he reached the danger
point, if not before.

"I wonder how a fellow would go about it
any way," he thought.   "He couldn't make any
sentimental remarks, without being instantly
frozen.   She's like the Boston girls we read
about in the funny papers.   He couldn't give
her things, either, except flowers or books, or
sweets, or music.   She has more books than she

wants, because she reviews 'em for the paper,
and I don't think she's musical.   She doesn't
look like the candy fiends, and I imagine she'd
pitch a box of chocolates into the sad sea, or
give it to Hepsey.   There's nothing left but
flowers — and I suppose she wouldn't notice
'em.

"A man would have to teach her to like
him, and, on my soul, I don't know how he'd
do that.   Constant devotion wouldn't have
any effect—I doubt if she'd permit it; and a
fellow might stay away from her for six
months, without a sign from her.   I guess
she's cold—no, she isn't, either — eyes and
temper like hers don't go with the icebergs.

"I — that is, he couldn't take her out,
because there's no place to go.   It's different in the city, of course, but if he happened
to meet her in the country, as I've done ——

"Might ask her to drive, possibly, if I could
rent Alfred and Mamie for a few hours — no,
we'd have to have the day, for anything over
two miles, and that wouldn't be good form,
without a chaperone.   Not that she needs
one — she's equal to any emergency, I fancy.
Besides, she wouldn't go.   If I could get
those two plugs up the hill, without pushing

'em, gravity would take 'em back, but I could n't ask her to walk up the hill after the pleasure excursion was over. I don't believe a drive would entertain her.

"Perhaps she 'd like to fish — no, she would n't, for she said she did n't like worms. Might sail on the briny deep, except that there 's no harbour within ten miles, and she would n't trust her fair young life to me. She 'd be afraid I 'd drown her.

"I suppose the main idea is to cultivate a clinging dependence, but I 'd like to see the man who could woo any dependence from Miss Thorne. She holds her head like a thoroughbred touched with the lash. She said she was afraid of Carlton, but I guess she was just trying to be pleasant. I 'll tell him about it — no, I won't, for I said I would n't.

"I wish there was some other girl here for me to talk to, but I 'll be lucky if I can get along peaceably with the one already here. I 'll have to discover all her pet prejudices and be careful not to walk on any of 'em. There 's that crazy woman, for instance — I must n't allude to her, even respectfully, if I 'm to have any softening feminine influence about me before I go back to town. She did n't seem to believe I had any letter from Carlton — that's what comes of being careless.

"I shouldn't have told her that people said she had large feet and wore men's shoes. She's got a pretty foot; I noticed it particularly before I spoke. I suppose she didn't like that — most girls wouldn't, I guess, but she took it as a hunter takes a fence. Even after that, she said she'd help me be patient, and last night, when she said she'd read the papers to me — she was awfully sweet to me then.

"Perhaps she likes me a little bit — I hope so. She'd never care very much for anybody, though — she's too independent. She wouldn't even let me help her up the hill; I don't know whether it was independence, or whether she didn't want me to touch her. If we ever come to a place where she has to be helped, I suppose I'll have to put gloves on, or let her hold one end of a stick while I hang on to the other.

"Still she didn't take her hand away last night, when I grabbed it. Probably she was thinking about something else, and didn't notice. It's a particularly nice hand to hold, but I'll never have another chance, I guess.

"Carlton said she'd take the conceit out of me, if I had any. I'm glad he didn't put that in the letter—still it doesn't matter, since I've lost it. I wish I hadn't, for what he said about me was really very nice. Carlton is a good fellow.

"How she lit on me when I thought the crazy person might make a good special! Jerusalem! I felt like the dust under her feet. I'd be glad to have anybody stand up for me, like that, but nobody ever will. She's mighty pretty when she's angry, but I'd rather she wouldn't get huffy at me. She's a tremendously nice girl—there's no doubt of that."

At this juncture, Joe came out on the porch, hat in hand. "Mornin', Mr. Winfield."

"Good morning, Joe; how are your troubles this morning?"

"They're all right, I guess," he replied, pleased with the air of comradeship. "Want me to read the paper to yer?"

"No, thank you, Joe, not this morning."

The tone was a dismissal, but Joe lingered, shifting from one foot to the other. "Ain't I done it to suit yer?"

"Quite so," returned Winfield, serenely.

"I don't mind doin' it," Joe continued,

after a long silence. "I won't charge yer nothin ."

"You 're very kind, Joe, but I don't care about it to-day." Winfield rose and walked to the other end of the porch. The apple trees were in bloom, and every wandering wind was laden with sweetness. Even the gnarled old tree in Miss Hathaway's yard, that had been out of bearing for many a year, had put forth a bough of fragrant blossoms. He saw it from where he stood; a mass of pink and white against the turquoise sky, and thought that Miss Thorne would make a charming picture if she stood beneath the tree with the blown petals drifting around her.

He lingered upon the vision till Joe spoke again. "Be you goin' up to Miss Hathaway's this mornin' ?"

"Why, I don't know," Winfield answered somewhat resentfully, "why ?"

"'Cause I would n't go — not if I was in your place."

"Why ?" he demanded, facing him.

"Miss Hathaway's niece, she 's sick."

"Sick!" repeated Winfield, in sudden fear, "what 's the matter!"

"Oh, 't ain't nothin' serious, I reckon, cause

she 's up and around.   I 've just come from
there, and Hepsey said that all night Miss
Thorne was a-cryin', and that this mornin' she
would n't eat no breakfast.   She don't never
eat much, but this mornin' she would n't eat
nothin', and she would n't say what was
wrong with her."

Winfield's face plainly showed his concern.

"She would n't eat nothin' last night, neither," Joe went on.   "Hepsey told me this
mornin' that she thought p'raps you and her
had fit.   She 's your girl, ain't she ?"

"No," replied Winfield, "she is n't my
girl, and we have n't 'fit.'   I 'm sorry she
is n't well."

He paced back and forth moodily, while
Joe watched him in silence.   "Well," he
said, at length, "I reckon I 'll be movin' along.
I just thought I 'd tell yer."

There was no answer, and Joe slammed the
gate in disgust.   "I wonder what 's the matter," thought Winfield.   "'T is n't a letter, for
to-day's mail has n't come and she was all
right last night.   Perhaps she is n't ill — she
said she cried when she was angry.   Great
Heavens!   I hope she is n't angry at me!

"She was awfully sweet to me just before

I left her," he continued, mentally, "so I'm not to blame. I wonder if she's angry at herself because she offered to read the papers to me?"

All unknowingly he had arrived at the cause of Miss Thorne's unhappiness. During a wakeful, miserable night, she had wished a thousand times that she might take back those few impulsive words.

"That must be it," he thought, and then his face grew tender. "Bless her sweet heart," he muttered, apropos of nothing, "I'm not going to make her unhappy. It's only her generous impulse, and I won't let her think it's any more."

The little maiden of his dreams was but a faint image just then, as he sat down to plan a course of action which would assuage Miss Thorne's tears. A grey squirrel appeared on the gate post, and sat there, calmly, cracking a nut.

He watched the little creature, absently, and then strolled toward the gate. The squirrel seemed tame and did not move until he was almost near enough to touch it, and then it scampered only a little way.

"I'll catch it," Winfield said to himself,

"and take it up to Miss Thorne. Perhaps she 'll be pleased."

It was simple enough, apparently, for the desired gift was always close at hand. He followed it across the hill, and bent a score of times to pick it up, but it was a guileful squirrel and escaped with great regularity.

Suddenly, with a flaunt of its bushy tail and a daring, backward glance, it scampered under the gate into Miss Ainslie's garden and Winfield laughed aloud. He had not known he was so near the other house and was about to retreat when something stopped him.

Miss Ainslie stood in the path just behind the gate, with her face ghastly white and her eyes wide with terror, trembling like a leaf. There was a troubled silence, then she said, thickly, "Go!"

"I beg your pardon," he answered, hurriedly, "I did not mean to frighten you."

"Go!" she said again, her lips scarcely moving, "Go!"

"Now what in the mischief have I done;" he thought, as he crept away, feeling like a thief. "I understood that this was a quiet place and yet the strenuous life seems to have struck the village in good earnest.

"What am I, that I should scare the aged
and make the young weep? I've always
been considered harmless, till now. That
must be Miss Thorne's friend, whom I met
so unfortunately just now. She's crazy,
surely, or she wouldn't have been afraid of
me. Poor thing, perhaps I startled her."

He remembered that she had carried a
basket and worn a pair of gardening gloves.
Even though her face was so changed, for an
instant he had seen its beauty—the deep violet eyes, fair skin, and regular features, sur-
mounted by that wonderful crown of silvered
hair.

Conflicting emotions swayed him as he
wended his way to the top of the hill, with
the morning paper in his pocket as an excuse,
if he should need one. When he approached
the gate, he was seized by a swift and unex-
plainable fear, and would have turned back,
but Miss Hathaway's door was opened.

Then the little maiden of his dreams
vanished, waving her hand in token of eternal
farewell, for as Ruth came down the path between the white and purple plumes of lilac, with
a smile of welcome upon her lips, he knew that,
in all the world, there was nothing half so fair.

VIII

Summer Days

THE rumble of voices which came from the kitchen was not disturbing, but when the rural lovers began to sit on the piazza, directly under Ruth's window, she felt called upon to remonstrate.

"Hepsey," she asked, one morning, "why don't you and Joe sit under the trees at the side of the house? You can take your chairs out there."

"Miss Hathaway allers let us set on the piazzer," returned Hepsey, unmoved.

"Miss Hathaway probably sleeps more soundly than I do. You don't want me to hear everything you say, do you?"

Hepsey shrugged her buxom shoulders. "You can if you like, mum."

"But I don't like," snapped Ruth. "It annoys me."

There was an interval of silence, then

Hepsey spoke again, of her own accord.
"If Joe and me was to set anywheres but in
front, he might see the light."

"Well, what of it?"

"Miss Hathaway, she don't want it talked
of, and men folks never can keep secrets,"
Hepsey suggested.

"You wouldn't have to tell him, would
you?"

"Yes 'm.   Men folks has got terrible curi-
ous minds.   They're all right if they don't
know there's nothin', but if they does, why
they's keen."

"Perhaps you're right, Hepsey, she replied, biting her lips.   "Sit anywhere you
please."

There were times when Ruth was compelled to admit that Hepsey's mental gifts
were fully equal to her own.   It was unreasonable to suppose, even for an instant,
that Joe and Hepsey had not pondered long
and earnestly upon the subject of the light in
the attic window, yet the argument was un-
answerable.   The matter had long since lost
its interest for Ruth — perhaps because she
was too happy to care.

Winfield had easily acquired the habit of

bringing her his morning papers, and, after the first embarrassment, Ruth settled down to it in a businesslike way. Usually, she sat in Miss Hathaway's sewing chair, under a tree a little way from the house, that she might at the same time have a general supervision of her domain, while Winfield stretched himself upon the grass at her feet. When the sun was bright, he wore his dark glasses, thereby gaining an unfair advantage.

After breakfast, which was a movable feast at the "Widder's," he went after his mail and brought hers also. When he reached the top of the hill, she was always waiting for him.

"This devotion is very pleasing," he remarked, one morning.

"Some people are easily pleased," she retorted. "I dislike to spoil your pleasure, but my stern regard for facts compels me to say that it is not Mr. Winfield I wait for, but the postman."

"Then I'll always be your postman, for I 'do admire' to be waited for, as they have it at the 'Widder's.' Of course, it's more or less of an expense — this morning, for instance, I had to dig up two cents to get one of your valuable manuscripts out of the clutches of an interested government."

"That's nothing," she assured him, "for I save you a quarter every day, by taking Joe's place as reader to Your Highness, not to mention the high tariff on the Sunday papers. Besides, the manuscripts are all in now."

"I'm glad to hear that," he replied, sitting down on the piazza. 'Do you know, Miss Thorne, I think there's a great deal of joyous excitement attached to the pursuit of literature. You send out a story, fondly believing that it is destined to make you famous. Time goes on, and you hear nothing from it. You can see your name 'featured' on the advertisements of the magazine, and hear the heavy tread of the fevered mob, on the way to buy up the edition. In the roseate glow of your fancy, you can see not only your cheque, but the things you're going to buy with it. Perhaps you tell your friends, cautiously, that you're writing for such and such a magazine. Before your joy evaporates, the thing comes back from the Dead Letter Office, because you had n't put on enough postage, and they would n't take it in. Or, perhaps they've written 'Return' on the front page in blue pencil, and all over it are little, dark, four-fingered prints, where the office pup has walked on it."

"You seem to be speaking from experience."

"You have guessed it, fair lady, with your usual wonderful insight. Now let 's read the paper — do you know, you read much better than Joe does?"

"Really?" Ruth was inclined to be sarcastic, but there was a delicate colour in her cheeks, which pleased his æsthetic sense.

At first, he had had an insatiable thirst for everything in the paper, except the advertisements. The market reports were sacrificed inside of a week, and the obituary notices, weather indications, and foreign despatches soon followed. Later, the literary features were eliminated, but the financial and local news died hard. By the end of June, however, he was satisfied with the headlines.

"No, thank you, I don't want to hear about the murder," he said, in answer to Ruth's ironical question, "nor yet the Summer styles in sleeves. All that slop on the Woman's Page, about making home happy, is not suited to such as I, and I 'll pass."

"There's a great deal here that's very interesting," returned Ruth, "and I doubt if I myself could have crammed more solid knowledge into one Woman's Page. Here's a full account of a wealthy lady's Summer home, and a description of a poor woman's garden, and eight recipes, and half a column on how to keep a husband at home nights, and plans for making a china closet out of an old bookcase."

"If there's anything that makes me dead tired," remarked Winfield, "it's that home-made furniture business."

"For once, we agree," answered Ruth. "I've read about it till I'm completely out of patience. Shirtwaist boxes from soap boxes, dressing tables from packing boxes, couches from cots, hall lamps from old arc light globes, and clothes hampers from barrels — all these I endured, but the last straw was a 'transformed kitchen.'"

"Tell me about it," begged Winfield, who was enjoying himself hugely.

"The stove was to be set into the wall," began Ruth, "and surrounded with marble and white tiling, or, if this was too expensive, it was to be hidden from view by a screen of

Japanese silk.   A nice oak settle, hand carved,
which 'the young husband might make in his
spare moments,' was to be placed in front of
it, and there were to be plate racks and
shelves on the walls, to hold the rare china.
Charming kitchen! "

Her cheeks were flushed and her eyes shone
like stars.   "You're an awfully funny girl,"
said Winfield, quietly, "to fly into a passion
over a ' transformed kitchen ' that you never
saw.   Why don't you save your temper for
real things ? "

She looked at him, meaningly, and he retreated in good order.   " I think I 'm a tactful
person," he continued, hurriedly, "because I
get on so well with you.   Most of the time,
we 're as contented as two kittens in a basket."

" My dear Mr. Winfield," returned Ruth,
pleasantly, "you 're not only tactful, but
modest.   I never met a man whose tempera-
ment so nearly approached the unassuming
violet.   I 'm afraid you 'll never be ap-
preciated in this world — you 're too good for
it.   You must learn to put yourself forward.
I expect it will be a shock to your sensitive
nature, but it 's got to be done."

" Thank you," he laughed.   " I wish we

were in town now, and I'd begin to put myself forward by asking you out to dinner and
afterward to the theatre."

"Why don't you take me out to dinner
here?" she asked.

"I wouldn't insult you by offering you the
'Widder's' cooking. I mean a real dinner,
with striped ice cream at the end of it."

"I'll go," she replied, "I can't resist the
blandishments of striped ice cream."

"Thank you again; that gives me courage
to speak of something that has lain very near
my heart for a long time."

"Yes?" said Ruth, conventionally. For
the moment she was frightened.

"I've been thinking fondly of your chafing-
dish, though I haven't been allowed to see it
yet, and I suppose there's nothing in the
settlement to cook in it, is there?"

"Nothing much, surely."

"We might have some stuff sent out from
the city, don't you think so?"

"Canned things?"

"Yes — anything that would keep."

Aided and abetted by Winfield, she made
out a list of articles which were unknown to
the simple-minded inhabitants of the village.

"I'll attend to the financial part of it," he
said, pocketing the list, "and then, my life
will be in your hands."

After he went away, Ruth wished she
knew more about the gentle art of cooking,
which, after all, is closely allied to the other
one — of making enemies. She decided to
dispense with Hepsey's services, when Winfield came up to dinner, and to do everything
herself.

She found an old cook book of Aunt Jane's
and turned over its pages with new interest.
It was in manuscript form, and seemed to
represent the culinary knowledge of the entire
neighbourhood. Each recipe was duly ac-
credited to its original author, and there were
many newspaper clippings, from the despised
"Woman's Page" in various journals.

Ruth thought it would be an act of kindness to paste the loose clippings into Aunt
Jane's book, and she could look them over as
she fastened them in. The work progressed
rapidly, until she found a clipping which was
not a recipe. It was a perfunctory notice of
the death of Charles Winfield, dated almost
eighteen years ago.

She remembered the various emotions old

newspapers had given her when she first came to Aunt Jane's. This was Abigail Weatherby's husband — he had survived her by a dozen years. "I'm glad it's Charles Winfield instead of Carl," thought Ruth, as she put it aside, and went on with her work.

"Pantry's come," announced Winfield, a few days later; "I did n't open it, but I think everything is there. Joe's going to bring it up."

"Then you can come to dinner Sunday," answered Ruth, smiling.

"I'll be here," returned Winfield promptly. "What time do we dine?"

"I don't know exactly. It's better to wait, I think, until Hepsey goes out. She always regards me with more or less suspicion, and it makes me uncomfortable."

Sunday afternoon, the faithful Joe drove up to the gate, and Hepsey emerged from her small back room, like a butterfly from a chrysalis. She was radiant in a brilliant blue silk, which was festooned at irregular intervals with white silk lace. Her hat was bending beneath its burden of violets and red roses, starred here and there with some unhappy buttercups which had survived the wreck of a previous millinery triumph. Her hands were encased in white cotton gloves, which did not fit.

With Joe's assistance, she entered the vehicle and took her place proudly on the back seat, even while he pleaded for her to sit beside him.

"You know yourself that I can't drive nothin' from the back seat," he complained.

"Nobody 's askin' you to drive nothin' from nowhere," returned Hepsey, scornfully. "If you can't take me out like a lady, I ain't a-goin'."

Ruth was dazzled by the magnificence of the spectacle and was unable to take her eyes away from it, even after Joe had turned around and started down hill. She thought Winfield would see them pass his door and time his arrival accordingly, so she was startled when he came up behind her and said, cheerfully:

"They look like a policeman's, don't they?"

"What—who?"

"Hepsey's hands—did you think I meant yours?"

"How long have you been here?"

"Nearly thirty years."

"That was n't what I meant," said Ruth, colouring. "How long have you been at Aunt Jane's?"

"Oh, that 's different. When Joe went out to harness his fiery steeds to his imposing chariot, I went around through the woods, across the beach, climbed a vertical precipice, and came up this side of the hill. I had to wait some little time, but I had a front seat during the show."

He brought out her favourite chair, placing it under the maple tree, then sat down near her. "I should think you 'd get some clothes like Hepsey's," he began. "I 'll wager, now, that you have n't a gown like that in your entire wardrobe."

"You 're right — I have n't. The nearest approach to it is a tailored gown, lined with silk, which Hepsey thinks I should wear wrong side out."

"How long will the coast be clear?"

"Until nine o'clock, I think. They go to church in the evening."

"It 's half past three now," he observed, glancing at his watch. "I had fried salt pork, fried eggs, and fried potatoes for breakfast.

I've renounced coffee, for I can't seem to get used to theirs. For dinner, we had round steak, fried, more fried potatoes, and boiled onions. Dried apple pie for dessert—I think I'd rather have had the mince I refused this morning."

"I'll feed you at five o'clock," she said, smiling.

"That seems like a long time," he complained.

"It won't, after you begin to entertain me."

It was after five before either realised it. "Come on," she said, "you can sit in the kitchen and watch me."

He professed great admiration while she put on one of Hepsey's white aprons, and when she appeared with the chafing-dish, his emotion was beyond speech. He was allowed to open the box and to cut up some button mushrooms, while she shredded cold chicken. "I'm getting hungry every minute," he said, "and if there is undue postponement, I fear I shall assimilate all the raw material in sight —including the cook."

Ruth laughed happily. She was making a sauce with real cream, seasoned delicately with paprika and celery salt. "Now I'll put in the chicken and mushrooms," she said, "and you can stir it while I make toast."

They were seated at the table in the dining-room and the fun was at its height, when they became aware of a presence. Hepsey stood in the door, apparently transfixed with surprise, and with disapproval evident in every line of her face. Before either could speak, she was gone.

Though Ruth was very much annoyed, the incident seemingly served to accentuate Win-field's enjoyment. The sound of wheels on the gravel outside told them that she was continuing her excursion.

"I'm going to discharge her to-morrow," Ruth said.

"You can't—she is in Miss Hathaway's service, not yours. Besides, what has she done? She came back, probably, after something she had forgotten. You have no reasonable ground for discharging her, and I think you'd be more uncomfortable if she went than if she stayed."

"Perhaps you're right," she admitted.

"I know how you feel about it," he went on, "but I hope you won't let her distress you. It does n't make a bit of difference to me; she's only amusing. Please don't bother about it."

"I won't," said Ruth, "that is, I'll try not to."

They piled the dishes in the sink, "as a pleasant surprise for Hepsey," he said, and the hours passed as if on wings. It was almost ten o'clock before it occurred to Winfield that his permanent abode was not Miss Hathaway's parlour.

As they stood at the door, talking, the last train came in. "Do you know," said Winfield, "that every night, just as that train comes in, your friend down there puts a candle in her front window?"

"Well," rejoined Ruth, sharply, "what of it? It's a free country, is n't it?"

"Very. Untrammelled press and highly independent women. Good night, Miss Thorne. I'll be up the first thing in the morning."

She was about to speak, but slammed the door instead, and was displeased when she heard a smothered laugh from outside.

IX

By Humble Means

AS lightly as a rose petal up⌐n the shimmering surface of a stream, Summer was
drifting away, but whither, no one seemed to
care. The odour of printer's ink upon the
morning paper no longer aroused vain longings
in Winfield's breast, and Ruth had all but
forgotten her former connection with the
newspaper world.

By degrees, Winfield had arranged a routine
which seemed admirable. Until luncheon
time, he was with Ruth and, usually, out of
doors, according to prescription. In the afternoon, he went up again, sometimes staying
to dinner, and, always, he spent his evenings
there.

"Why don't you ask me to have my trunk
sent up here?" he asked Ruth, one day.

"I had n't thought of it," she laughed. "I
suppose it has n't seemed necessary."

"Miss Hathaway would be pleased, would n't she, if she knew she had two guests instead of one ?"

" Undoubtedly; how could she help it ?"

"When do you expect her to return ?"

"I don't know—I have n't heard a word from her. Sometimes I feel a little anxious about her." Ruth would have been much concerned for her relative's safety, had she known that the eccentric lady had severed herself from the excursion and gone boldly into Italy, unattended, and with no knowledge of the language.

Hepsey inquired daily for news of Miss Hathaway, but no tidings were forthcoming. She amused herself in her leisure moments by picturing all sorts of disasters in which her mistress was doubtless engulfed, and in speculating upon the tie between Miss Thorne and Mr. Winfield.

More often than not, it fell to Hepsey to light the lamp in the attic window, though she did it at Miss Thorne's direction. "If I forget it, Hepsey," she had said, calmly, "you 'll see to it, won't you ?"

Trunks, cedar chests, old newspapers, and long hidden letters were out of Ruth's pro-

vince now. Once in two or three weeks, she
went to see Miss Ainslie, but never stayed
long, though almost every day she reproached
herself for neglect.

Winfield's days were filled with peace,
since he had learned how to get on with Miss
Thorne. When she showed herself stubborn
and unyielding, he retreated gracefully, and
with a suggestion of amusement, as a courtier
may step aside gallantly for an angry lady to
pass. Ruth felt his mental attitude and, even
though she resented it, she was ashamed.

Having found that she could have her
own way, she became less anxious for it,
and several times made small concessions,
which were apparently unconscious, but
amusing, nevertheless. She had none of the
wiles of the coquette; she was transparent,
and her friendliness was disarming. If she
wanted Winfield to stay at home any particular morning or afternoon, she told him so. At
first he was offended, but afterward learned to
like it, for she could easily have instruc⁺ed
Hepsey to say that she was out.

The pitiless, unsympathetic calendar re-
corded the fact that July was near its end,
and Ruth sighed—then hated herself for it.

She had grown accustomed to idleness, and, under the circumstances, liked it far too well.

One morning, when she went down to breakfast, Hepsey was evidently perplexed about something, but Ruth took no outward note of it, knowing that it would be revealed ere long.

"Miss Thorne," she said, tentatively, as Ruth rose from the table.

"Yes?"

"Of course, Miss Thorne, I reckon likely 't ain't none of my business, but is Mr. Winfield another detective, and have you found anything out yet?"

Ruth, inwardly raging, forced herself to let the speech pass unnoticed, and sailed majestically out of the room. She was surprised to discover that she could be made so furiously angry by so small a thing.

Winfield was coming up the hill with the mail, and she tried to cool her hot cheeks with her hands. "Let's go down on the side of the hill," she said, as he gave her some letters and the paper; "it's very warm in the sun, and I'd like the sea breeze."

They found a comparatively level place, with two trees to lean against, and, though

they were not far from the house, they were
effectually screened by the rising ground.
Ruth felt that she could not bear the sight of
Hepsey just then.

After glancing at her letters she began to
read aloud, with a troubled haste which did
not escape him. "Here's a man who had a
little piece of bone taken out of the inside of
his skull," she said. "Shall I read about that?
He seems, literally, to have had something on
his mind."

"You're brilliant this morning," answered
Winfield, gravely, and she laughed hysteri-
cally.

"What's the matter with you?" he asked.
"You don't seem like yourself."

"It isn't nice of you to say that," she retorted, "considering your previous remark."

There was a rumble and a snort on the road
and, welcoming the diversion, he went up to
reconnoitre. "Joe's coming; is there anything you want in the village?"

"No," she answered, wearily, "there's
nothing I want — anywhere."

"You're an exceptional woman," returned
Winfield, promptly, "and I'd advise you to
sit for your photograph. The papers would

like it — ' Picture of the Only Woman Who Does n't Want Anything — why, that would work off an extra in about ten minutes! "

Ruth looked at him for a moment, then turned her eyes away. He felt vaguely uncomfortable, and was about to offer atonement when Joe's deep bass voice called out: " Hello! "

" Hello yourself! " came in Hepsey's highest tones, from the garden.

" Want anything to-day ? "

" Nope ! "

There was a brief pause, and then Joe shouted again: " Hepsey! "

" Well ? "

" I should think they 'd break their vocal cords," said Winfield.

" I wish they would," rejoined Ruth, quickly.

" Come here! " yelled Joe. " I want to talk to yer."

" Talk from there," screamed Hepsey.

" Where 's yer folks ? "

" D' know."

" Say, be they courtin' ? "

Hepsey left her work in the garden and came toward the front of the house. " They

walk out some," she said, when she was half-
way to the gate, "and they set up a good
deal, and Miss Thorne told me she did n't
know as she'd do better, but you can't rightly
say they're courtin' 'cause city ways ain't like
our 'n."

The deep colour dyed Ruth's face and her
hands twitched nervously. Winfield very
much desired to talk, but could think of
nothing to say. The situation was tense.

Joe clucked to his horses. "So long," he
said. "See yer later."

Ruth held her breath until he passed them,
and then broke down. Her self control was
quite gone, and she sobbed bitterly, in grief
and shame. Winfield tucked his handkerchief
into her cold hands, not knowing what else
to do.

"Don't!" he said, as if he, too, had been
hurt. "Ruth, dear, don't cry!"

A new tenderness almost unmanned him,
but he sat still with his hands clenched, feeling like a brute because of her tears.

The next few minutes seemed like an hour,
then Ruth raised her head and tried to smile.
"I expect you think I'm silly," she said,
hiding her tear stained face again.

"No!" he cried, sharply; then, with a catch in his throat, he put his hand on her shoulder.

"Don't!" she sobbed, turning away from him, "what—what they said—was bad enough!"

The last words ended in a rush of tears, and, sorely distressed, he began to walk back and forth. Then a bright idea came to him. "I'll be back in a minute," he said.

When he returned, he had a tin dipper, freshly filled with cold water. "Don't cry any more," he pleaded, gently, "I'm going to bathe your face."

Ruth leaned back against the tree and he knelt beside her. "Oh, that feels so good," she said, gratefully, as she felt his cool fingers upon her burning eyes. In a little while she was calm again, though her breast still heaved with every fluttering breath.

"You poor little woman," he said, tenderly, "you're just as nervous as you can be. Don't feel so about it. Just suppose it was somebody who wasn't!"

"Who wasn't what?" asked Ruth, innocently.

Winfield crimsoned to the roots of his hair and hurled the dipper into the distance.

"What — what — they said," he stammered, sitting down awkwardly. "Oh, darn it!" He kicked savagely at a root, and added, in bitterest self accusation, "I'm a chump, I am!"

"No you're not," returned Ruth, with sweet shyness, "you're nice. Now we'll read some more of the paper."

He assumed a feverish interest in the market reports, but his thoughts were wandering. Certainly, nothing could have been worse. He felt as if a bud, which he had been long and eagerly watching, was suddenly torn open by a vandal hand. When he first touched Ruth's eyes with his finger tips, he had trembled like a schoolboy, and he wondered if she knew it.

If she did, she made no sign. Her cheeks were flushed, the lids of her downcast eyes were pink, and her voice had lost its crisp, incisive tones, but she read rapidly, without comment or pause, until the supply of news gave out. Then she began on the advertisements, dreading the end of her task and vainly wishing for more papers, though in her heart there was something sweet, which, even to herself, she dared not name.

"That 'll do," he said, abruptly, "I 'm not interested in the 'midsummer glove clearing.' I meant to tell you something when I first came — I 've got to go away."

Ruth's heart throbbed painfully, as if some cold hand held it fast. "Yes," she said, politely, not recognising her own voice.

"It 's only for a week — I 've got to go to the oculist and see about some other things. I 'll be back before long."

"I shall miss you," she said, conventionally. Then she saw that he was going away to relieve her from the embarrassment of his presence, and blessed him accordingly.

"When are you going?" she asked.

"This afternoon. I don't want to go, but it 's just as well to have it over with. Can I do anything for you in the city?"

"No, thank you. My wants are few and, at present, well supplied."

"Don't you want me to match something for you? I thought women always had pieces of stuff that had to be matched immediately."

"They made you edit the funny column, did n't they?" she asked, irrelevantly.

"They did, Miss Thorne, and, moreover, I expect I 'll have to do it again."

After a little, they were back on the old footing, yet everything was different, for there was an obtruding self consciousness on either side. "What time do you go?" she asked, with assumed indifference.

"Three-fifteen, I think, and it's after one now."

He walked back to the house with her, and, for the second time that day, Hepsey came out to sweep the piazza.

"Good bye, Miss Thorne," he said.

"Good bye, Mr. Winfield."

That was all, but Ruth looked up with an unspoken question and his eyes met hers clearly, with no turning aside. She knew he would come back very soon and she understood his answer — that he had the right.

As she entered the house, Hepsey said, pleasantly: "Has he gone away, Miss Thorne?"

"Yes," she answered, without emotion. She was about to say that she did not care for luncheon, then decided that she must seem to care.

Still, it was impossible to escape that keen-eyed observer. "You ain't eatin' much," she suggested.

"I'm not very hungry."

"Be you sick, Miss Thorne?"

"No—not exactly. I've been out in the sun and my head aches," she replied, clutching at the straw.

"Do you want a wet rag?"

Ruth laughed, remembering an earlier suggestion of Winfield's. "No, I don't want any wet rag, Hepsey, but I'll go up to my room for a little while, I think. Please don't disturb me."

She locked her door, shutting out all the world from the nameless joy that surged in her heart. The mirror disclosed flushed, feverish cheeks and dark eyes that shone like stars. "Ruth Thorne," she said to herself, "I'm ashamed of you! First you act like a fool and then like a girl of sixteen!"

Then her senses became confused and the objects in the room circled around her unsteadily. "I'm tired," she murmured. Her head sank drowsily into the lavender scented pillow and she slept too soundly to take note of the three o'clock train leaving the station. It was almost sunset when she was aroused by voices under her window.

"That feller's gone home," said Joe.

"Do tell!" exclaimed Hepsey. "Did he pay his board?"

"Yep, every cent. He's a-comin' back."

"When?"

"D' know. Don't she know?" The emphasis indicated Miss Thorne.

"I guess not," answered Hepsey. "They said good bye right in front of me, and there wa'n't nothin' said about it."

"They ain't courtin', then," said Joe, after a few moments of painful thought, and Ruth, in her chamber above, laughed happily to herself.

"Mebbe not," rejoined Hepsey. "It ain't fer sech as me to say when there's courtin' and when there ain't, after havin' gone well nigh onto five year with a country loafer what ain't never said nothin'." She stalked into the house, closed the door, and noisily bolted it. Joe stood there for a moment, as one struck dumb, then gave a long, low whistle of astonishment and walked slowly down the hill.

X

Love Letters

"A WEEK!" Ruth said to herself the next morning. "Seven long days! No letter, because he must n't write, no telegram, because there's no office within ten miles — nothing to do but wait!"

When she went down to breakfast, Hepsey did not seem to hear her cheery greeting, but was twisting her apron and walking about restlessly. "Miss Thorne," she said, at length, "did you ever get a love letter?"

"Why, yes, of course," laughed Ruth. "Every girl gets love letters."

Hepsey brightened visibly, then inquired, with great seriousness: "Can you read writin', Miss Thorne?"

"That depends on the writing."

"Yes'm, it does so. I can read some writin'—I can read Miss Hathaway's writin', and some of the furrin letters she's had, but

I got some this mornin' I can't make out, nohow."

"Where did you find 'writing' this morning? It's too early for the mail, is n't it?"

"Yes'm. It was stuck under the kitchen
winder." Hepsey looked up at the ceiling in
an effort to appear careless, and sighed. Then
she clutched violently at the front of her blue
gingham dress, immediately repenting of her
rashness. Ruth was inwardly amused but
asked no helpful questions.

Finally, Hepsey took the plunge. "Would
you mind tryin' to make out some writin' I 've
got, Miss Thorne?"

"Of course not — let me see it."

Hepsey extracted a letter from the inmost
recesses of her attire and stood expectantly,
with her hands on her hips.

"Why, it's a love letter!" Ruth exclaimed.

"Yes'm. When you get through readin'
it to yourself, will you read it out loud?"

The letter, which was written on ruled
note paper, bore every evidence of care and
thought. "Hepsey," it began, and, on the
line below, with a great flourish under it,
"Respected Miss" stood, in large capitals.

"Although it is now but a short interval,"

Ruth read, "since my delighted eyes first rested on your beautiful form ——"

"Five year!" interjected Hepsey.

"—— yet I dare to hope that you will receive graciously what I am about to say, as I am assured you will, if you reciprocate the sentiments which you have aroused in my bosom.

"In this short time, dear Miss, brief though it is, yet it has proved amply sufficient for my heart to go out to you in a yearning love which I have never before felt for one of your sex. Day by day and night by night your glorious image has followed me."

"That's a lie," interrupted Hepsey, "he knows I never chased him nowheres, not even when he took that red-headed Smith girl to the Sunday-school picnic over to the Ridge, a year ago come August."

"Those dark tresses have entwined my soul in their silken meshes, those deep eyes, that have borrowed their colour from Heaven's cerulean blue, and those soft white hands, that have never been roughened by uncongenial toil, have been ever present in my dreams."

Ruth paused for a moment, overcome by her

task, but Hepsey's face was radiant. "Hurry up, Miss Thorne," she said, impatiently.

"In short, Dear Miss, I consider you the most surpassingly lovely of your kind, and it is with pride swelling in my manly bosom that I dare to ask so peerless a jewel for her heart and hand.

"My parentage, birth, and breeding are probably known to you, but should any points remain doubtful, I will be pleased to present references as to my character and standing in the community.

"I await with impatience, Madam, your favourable answer to my plea. Rest assured that if you should so honour me as to accept my proposal, I will endeavour to stand always between you and the hard, cruel world, as your faithful shield. I will also endeavour constantly to give you a happiness as great as that which will immediately flood my being upon receipt of your blushing acceptance.

"I remain, Dear Miss, your devoted lover and humble servant,

"JOSEPH PENDLETON, ESQ."

"My! My!" ejaculated Hepsey. "Ain't that fine writin'!"

"It certainly is," responded Miss Thorne, keeping her face straight with difficulty.

"Would you mind readin' it again?"

She found the second recital much easier, since she was partially accustomed to the heavy punctuation marks and shaded flourishes. At first, she had connected Winfield with the effusion, but second thought placed the blame where it belonged — at the door of a "Complete Letter Writer."

"Miss Thorne," said Hepsey, hesitating.

"Yes?"

"Of course, I'd like my answer to be as good writin' as his'n."

"Naturally."

"Where d' you s'pose he got all that lovely grammar?"

"Grammar is a rare gift, Hepsey."

"Yes'm, 't is so. Miss Thorne, do you guess you could write as good as that?"

"I'd be willing to try," returned Ruth, with due humility.

Hepsey thought painfully for a few moments. "I d' know jest what I'd better say. Now, last night, I give Joe a hint, as you may say, but I wouldn't want him to think I'd jest been a-waitin' for him."

" No, of course not."

" Ain't it better to keep him in suspense, as you may say ?"

" Far better, Hepsey; he 'll think more of you."

" Then I 'll jest write that I 'm willin' to think it over, and if you 'll put it on a piece of paper fer me, I 'll write it out with ink. I 've got two sheets of paper jest like this, with nice blue lines onto it, that I 've been a-savin' fer a letter, and Miss Hathaway, she 's got ink."

Ruth sat down to compose an answer which should cast a shadow over the " Complete Letter Writer." Her pencil flew over the rough copy paper with lightning speed, while Hepsey stood by in amazement.

" Listen," she said, at length, " how do you like this ? "

" Mr. Joseph Pendleton—

" *Respected Sir :* Although your communication of recent date was a great surprise to me, candour compels me to confess that it was not entirely disagreeable. I have observed, though with true feminine delicacy, that your affections were inclined to settle in

my direction, and have not repelled your
advances.

"Still, I do not feel that as yet we are suffi-
ciently acquainted to render immediate matri-
mony either wise or desirable, and since the
suddenness of your proposal has in a measure
taken my breath away, I must beg that you
will allow me a proper interval in which to
consider the matter, and, in the meantime,
think of me simply as your dearest friend.

"I may add, in conclusion, that your character and standing in the community are entirely satisfactory to me.   Thanking you for
the honour you have conferred upon me, believe me, Dear Sir,

"Your sincere friend,

"HEPSEY."

"My!" exclaimed Hepsey, with overmas-
tering pride; "ain't that beautiful!   It's better than his'n, ain't it?"

"I would n't say that," Ruth replied, with
proper modesty, "but I think it will do."

"Yes'm.   'T will so.   Your writin' ain't
nothin' like Joe's," she continued, scanning it
closely, "but it's real pretty."   Then a bright
idea illuminated her countenance.   "Miss

Thorne, if you 'll **write** it out on the note paper with a pencil, I can go over it with the ink, and afterward, when it 's dry, I 'll rub out the pencil. It 'll be my writin' then, but it 'll look jest like yours."

" All right, Hepsey."

She found it difficult to follow the lines closely, but at length achieved a respectable result. "I 'll take good care of it," Hepsey said, wrapping the precious missive in a newspaper, "and this afternoon, when I get my work done up, I 'll fix it. **Joe** 'll be surprised, won't he?"

Late in the evening, when Hepsey came to Ruth, worn with the unaccustomed labours of correspondence, and proudly displayed the nondescript epistle, she was compelled to admit that unless Joe had superhuman qualities he would indeed " be surprised."

The next afternoon Ruth went down to Miss Ainslie's. "You 've been neglecting me, dear," said that gentle soul, as she opened the door.

"I have n't meant to," returned Ruth, conscience stricken, as she remembered how long it had been since the gate of the old-fashioned garden had swung on its hinges for her.

A quiet happiness had settled down upon Ruth and the old perturbed spirit was gone, but Miss Ainslie was subtly different. "I feel as if something was going to happen," she said.

"Something nice?"

"I — don't know." The sweet face was troubled and there were fine lines about the mouth, such as Ruth had never seen there before.

"You're nervous, Miss Ainslie — it's my turn to scold now."

"I never scolded you, did I deary?"

"You couldn't scold anybody — you're too sweet. You're not unhappy, are you, Miss Ainslie?"

"I? Why, no! Why should I be unhappy?" Her deep eyes were fixed upon Ruth.

"I — I didn't know," Ruth answered, in confusion.

"I learned long ago," said Miss Ainslie, after a little, "that we may be happy or not, just as we choose. Happiness is not a circumstance, nor a set of circumstances; it's only a light, and we may keep it burning if we will. So many of us are like children, crying for the moon, instead of playing contentedly with the few toys we have. We 're always hoping for something, and when it does n't come we fret and worry ; when it does, why there 's always something else we 'd rather have. We deliberately make nearly all of our unhappiness, with our own unreasonable discontent, and nothing will ever make us happy, deary, except the spirit within."

"But, Miss Ainslie," Ruth objected, "do you really think everybody can be happy ?"

"Of course — everybody who wishes to be. Some people are happier when they 're miserable. I don't mean, deary, that it 's easy for any of us, and it 's harder for some than for others, all because we never grow up. We 're always children — our playthings are a little different, that 's all."

"'Owning ourselves forever children,'" quoted Ruth, "'gathering pebbles on a boundless shore.'"

"Yes, I was just thinking of that. A little girl breaks her doll, and though the new one may be much prettier, it never wholly fills

the vacant place, and it 's that way with a
woman's dream." The sweet voice sank into
a whisper, followed by a lingering sigh.

"Miss Ainslie," said Ruth, after a pause,
"did you know my mother?"

"No, I did n't, deary—I 'm sorry. I saw
her once or twice, but she went away, soon
after we came here."

"Never mind," Ruth said, hurriedly, for
Mrs. Thorne's family had never forgiven her
runaway marriage.

"Come into the garden," Miss Ainslie suggested, and Ruth followed her, willingly, into
the cloistered spot where golden lilies tinkled,
thrushes sang, and every leaf breathed peace.

Miss Ainslie gathered a bit of rosemary,
crushing it between her white fingers.
"See," she said, "some of us are like that —
it takes a blow to find the sweetness in our
souls. Some of us need dry, hard places, like
the poppies"— pointing to a mass of brilliant
bloom — "and some of us are always thorny,
like the cactus, with only once in a while a
rosy star.

"I 've always thought my flowers had
souls, dear," she went on ; "they seem like
real people to me. I 've seen the roses rub-

bing their cheeks together as if they loved each other, and the forget-me-nots are little blue-eyed children, half afraid of the rest.

"Over there, it always seems to me as if the lavender was a little woman in a green dress, with a lavender bonnet and a white kerchief. She's one of those strong, sweet, wholesome people, who always rest you, and her sweetness lingers long after she goes away. I gather all the flowers, and every leaf, though the flowers are sweetest. I put the leaves away with my linen and the flowers among my laces. I have some beautiful lace, deary."

"I know you have—I've often admired it."

"I'm going to show it to you some day," she said, with a little quiver in her voice, "and some other day, when I can't wear it any more, you shall have some of it for your own."

"Don't, Miss Ainslie," cried Ruth, the quick tears coming to her eyes, "I don't want any lace—I want you!"

"I know," she answered, but there was a far-away look in her eyes, and something in her voice that sounded like a farewell.

"Miss Thorne," called Joe from the gate, "here's a package for yer. It come on the train."

He waited until Ruth went to him and seemed disappointed when she turned back into the garden. "Say," he shouted, "is Hepsey to home?"

Ruth was busy with the string and did not hear. "Oh, look!" she exclaimed, "what roses!"

"They're beautiful, deary. I do not think I have ever seen such large ones. Do you know what they are?"

"American Beauties — they're from Mr. Winfield. He knows I love them."

Miss Ainslie started violently. "From whom, dear?" she asked, in a strange tone.

"Mr. Winfield — he's going to be on the same paper with me in the Fall. He's here for the Summer, on account of his eyes."

Miss Ainslie was bending over the lavender. "It is a very common name, is it not?" she asked.

"Yes, quite common," answered Ruth, absently, taking the roses out of the box.

"You must bring him to see me some time, dear; I should like to know him."

"Thank you, Miss Ainslie, I will."

They stood at the gate together, and Ruth put a half blown rose into her hand. "I would n't give it to anybody but you," she said, half playfully, and then Miss Ainslie knew her secret. She put her hand on Ruth's arm and looked down into her face, as if there was something she must say.

"I don't forget the light, Miss Ainslie."

"I know," she breathed, in answer. She looked long and searchingly into Ruth's eyes, then whispered brokenly, "God bless you, dear. Good bye!"

XI

The Rose of all the World

"HE did n't forget me! He did n't forget me!" Ruth's heart sang in time with her step as she went home. Late afternoon flooded all the earth with gold, and from the other side of the hill came the gentle music of the sea.

The doors were open, but there was no trace of Hepsey. She put the roses in her water pitcher, and locked her door upon them as one hides a sacred joy. She went out again, her heart swelling like the throat of a singing bird, and walked to the brow of the cliff, with every sense keenly alive. Upon the surface of the ocean lay that deep, translucent blue which only Tadema has dared to paint.

"I must go down," she murmured.

Like a tawny ribbon trailed upon the green, the road wound down the hill. She followed it until she reached the side path on the right, and went down into the woods. The great boughs arched over her head like the nave of a cathedral, and the Little People of the Forest, in feathers and fur, scattered as she approached. Bright eyes peeped at her from behind tree trunks, or the safe shelter of branches, and rippling bird music ended in a frightened chirp.

"Oh," she said aloud, "don't be afraid!"

Was this love, she wondered, that lay upon her eyes like the dew of a Spring morning, that made the air vocal with rapturous song, and wrought white magic in her soul? It had all the mystery and freshness of the world's beginning; it was the rush of waters where sea and river meet, the perfume of a flower, and the far light trembling from a star. It was sunrise where there had been no day, the ecstasy of a thousand dawns; a new sun gleaming upon noon. All the joy of the world surged and beat in her pulses, till it seemed that her heart had wings.

Sunset came upon the water, the colour on the horizon reflecting soft iridescence upon the blue. Slow sapphire surges broke at her feet, tossing great pearls of spray against the cliff. Suddenly, as if by instinct, she turned — and faced Winfield.

"Thank you for the roses," she cried, with her face aglow.

He gathered her into his arms. "Oh, my Rose of All the World," he murmured, "have I found you at last?"

It was almost dusk when they turned to go home, with their arms around each other, as if they were the First Two, wandering through the shaded groves of Paradise, before sin came into the world.

"Did you think it would be like this?" she asked, shyly.

"No, I did n't, darling. I thought it would be very prim and proper. I never dreamed you 'd let me kiss you — yes, I did, too, but I thought it was too good to be true."

"I had to — to let you," she explained, crimsoning, "but nobody ever did before. I always thought — " Then Ruth hid her face against his shoulder, in maidenly shame.

When they came to the log across the path, they sat down, very close together. "You said we 'd fight if we came here," Ruth whispered.

"We're not going to, though. I want to tell you something, dear, and I have n't had the words for it till now."

"What is it?" she asked, in alarm.

"It's only that I love you, Ruth," he said, holding her closer, "and when I've said that, I've said all. It is n't an idle word; it's all my life that I give you, to do with as you will. It is n't anything that's apart from you, or ever could be; it's as much yours as your hands or eyes are. I did n't know it for a little while — that 's because I was blind. To think that I should go up to see you, even that first day, without knowing you for my sweetheart —my wife!"

"No, don't draw away from me. You little wild bird, are you afraid of Love? It's the sweetest thing God ever let a man dream of, Ruth —there's nothing like it in all the world. Look up, Sweet Eyes, and say you love me!"

Ruth's head drooped, and he put his hand under her chin, turning her face toward him, but her eyes were downcast still. "Say it, darling," he pleaded,

"I — I can't," she stammered.

"Why, dear?"

"Because — because — you know."

"I want you to say it, sweetheart.   Won't you?"

"Sometime, perhaps."

"When?"

"When — when it's dark."

"It's dark now."

"No it isn't.   How did you know?"

"How did I know what, dear?"

"That I—that I—cared."

"I knew the day you cried. I didn't know myself until then, but it all came in a minute."

"I was afraid you were going to stay away a whole week."

"I couldn't, darling — I just had to come."

"Did you see everybody you wanted to see?"

"I couldn't see anything but your face, Ruth, with the tears on it.   I've got to go back to-morrow and have another try at the oculist."

"Oh!" she exclaimed, in acute disappointment.

"It's the last time, sweetheart; we'll never be separated again."

"Never?"

"Never in all the world — nor afterward."

"I expect you think I'm silly," she said, wiping her eyes, as they rose to go home, "but I don't want you to go away."

"I don't want to go, dearest. If you're going to cry, you'll have me a raving maniac. I can't stand it, now."

"I'm not going to," she answered, smiling through her tears, "but it's a blessed privilege to have a nice stiff collar and a new tie to cry on."

"They're at your service, dear, for anything but that. I suppose we're engaged now, are n't we?"

"I don't know," said Ruth, in a low tone; "you have n't asked me to marry you."

"Do you want me to?"

"It's time, is n't it?"

Winfield bent over and whispered to her.

"I must think about it," said Ruth, very gravely, "it's so sudden."

"Oh, you sweet girl," he laughed, "are n't you going to give me any encouragement?"

"You've had some."

"I want another," he answered, purposely misunderstanding her, "and besides, it's dark now."

The sweet-scented twilight still lingered on the hillside, and a star or two gleamed through the open spaces above. A moment later, Ruth, in her turn, whispered to him. It was only a word or two, but the bright-eyed robins who were peeping at them from the maple branches must have observed that it was highly satisfactory.

XII

Bride and Groom

THOUGH Winfield had sternly determined
to go back to town the following day,
he did not achieve departure until later. Ruth
went to the station with him, and desolation
came upon her when the train pulled out, in
spite of the new happiness in her heart.

She had little time to miss him, however,
for, at the end of the week, and in accordance
with immemorial custom, the Unexpected
happened.

She was sitting at her window one morning, trying to sew, when the village chariot
stopped at the gate and a lady descended.
Joe stirred lazily on the front seat, but she
said, in a clear, high-pitched voice: "You
need n't trouble yourself, Joe. He 'll carry
the things."

She came toward the house, fanning herself
with a certain stateliness, and carrying her
handkerchief primly, by the exact centre of it.

In her wake was a little old gentleman, with a huge bundle, surrounded by a shawl-strap, a large valise, much the worse for wear, a telescope basket which was expanded to its full height, and two small parcels. A cane was tucked under one arm and an umbrella under the other. He could scarcely be seen behind the mountain of baggage.

Hepsey was already at the door. "Why, Miss Hathaway!" she cried, in astonishment.

"'T ain't Miss Hathaway," rejoined the visitor, with some asperity, "it's Mrs. Ball, and this is my husband. Niece Ruth, I presume," she added, as Miss Thorne appeared. "Ruth, let me introduce you to your Uncle James."

The bride was of medium height and rather angular. Her eyes were small, dark, and so piercingly brilliant that they suggested jet beads. Her skin was dark and her lips had been habitually compressed into a straight line. None the less, it was the face that Ruth had seen in the ambrotype at Miss Ainslie's, with the additional hardness that comes to those who grow old without love. Her bearing was that of a brisk, active woman, accustomed all her life to obedience and respect.

Mr. Ball was two or three inches shorter than his wife, and had a white beard, irregularly streaked with brown. He was bald-headed in front, had scant, reddish hair in the back, and his faded blue eyes were tearful. He had very small feet and the unmistakable gait of a sailor. Though there was no immediate resemblance, Ruth was sure that he was the man whose picture was in Aunt Jane's treasure chest in the attic. The daredevil look was gone, however, and he was merely a quiet, inoffensive old gentleman, for whom life had been none too easy.

"Welcome to your new home, James," said his wife, in a crisp, businesslike tone, which but partially concealed a latent tenderness. He smiled, but made no reply.

Hepsey still stood in the parlour, in wide mouthed astonishment, and it was Ruth's good fortune to see the glance which Mrs. Ball cast upon her offending maid. There was no change of expression except in the eyes, but Hepsey instantly understood that she was out of her place, and retreated to the kitchen with a flush upon her cheeks, which was altogether foreign to Ruth's experience.

"You can set here, James," resumed Mʳs. Ball, "until I have taken off my things."

The cherries on her black straw bonnet were shaking on their stems in a way which fascinated Ruth. "I'll take my things out of the south room, Aunty," she hastened to say.

"You won't, neither," was the unexpected answer; "that's the spare room, and, while you stay, you'll stay there."

Ruth was wondering what to say to her new uncle and sat in awkward silence as Aunt Jane ascended the stairs. Her step sounded lightly overhead and Mr. Ball twirled his thumbs absently.

"You—you've come a long way, have n't you?" she asked.

"Yes 'm, a long way." Then, seemingly for the first time, he looked at her, and a benevolent expression came upon his face. "You've got awful pretty hair, Niece Ruth," he observed, admiringly; "now Mis' Ball, she wears a false front."

The lady of the house returned at this juncture, with the false front a little askew. "I was just a-sayin'," Mr. Ball continued, "that our niece is a real pleasant lookin' woman."

"She 's your niece by marriage," his wife replied, "but she ain't no real relative."

"Niece by merriage is relative enough," said Mr. Ball, "and I say she 's a pleasant lookin' woman, ain't she, now?"

"She 'll do, I reckon. She resembles her Ma." Aunt Jane looked at Ruth, as if pitying the sister who had blindly followed the leadings of her heart and had died unforgiven.

"Why did n't you let me know you were coming, Aunt Jane?" asked Ruth. I 've been looking for a letter every day and I understood you were n't coming back until October."

"I trust I am not unwelcome in my own house," was the somewhat frigid response.

"No indeed, Aunty — I hope you 've had a pleasant time."

"We 've had a beautiful time, ain't we, James? We 've been on our honeymoon."

"Yes 'm, we hev been on our honeymoon, travellin' over strange lands an' furrin wastes of waters. Mis' Ball was terrible sea sick comin' here."

"In a way," said Aunt Jane, "we ain't completely married. We was married by a heathen priest in a heathen country and it ain't rightfully bindin', but we thought it would do until we could get back here and be married by a minister of the gospel, did n't we, James?"

"It has held," he said, without emotion, "but I reckon we will hev to be married proper."

"Likewise I have my weddin' dress," Aunt Jane went on, "what ain't never been worn. It 's a beautiful dress — trimmed with pearl trimmin' "— here Ruth felt the pangs of a guilty conscience — "and I lay out to be married in it, quite private, with you and Hepsey for witnesses."

"Why, it 's quite a romance, is n't it, Aunty?"

"'T is in a way," interjected Mr. Ball, "and in another way, 't ain't."

"Yes, Ruth," Aunt Jane continued, ignoring the interruption, "'t is a romance — a real romance," she repeated, with all the hard lines in her face softened. "We was engaged over thirty-five year. James went to sea to make a fortin', so he could give me every luxury. It 's all writ out in a letter I 've got upstairs. They 's beautiful letters, Ruth, and it 's come to me, as I 've been settin' here, that you might make a book out 'n these letters of James's. You write, don't you?"

"Why, yes, Aunty, I write for the papers, but I 've never done a book."

"Well, you 'll never write a book no earlier, and here 's all the material, as you may say, jest a-waitin' for you to copy it. I guess there 's over a hundred letters."

"But, Aunty," objected Ruth, struggling with inward emotion, "I could n't sign my name to it, you know, unless I had written the letters."

"Why not?"

"Because it would n't be honest," she answered, clutching at the straw, "the person who wrote the letters would be entitled to the credit—and the money," she added, hopefully.

"Why, yes, that 's right. Do you hear, James? It 'll have to be your book—'The Love Letters of a Sailor,' by James Ball, and dedicated in the front 'to my dearly beloved wife, Jane Ball, as was Jane Hathaway.' It 'll be beautiful, won't it, James?"

"Yes 'm, I hev no doubt but what it will."

"Do you remember, James, how you borrered a chisel from the tombstone man over

to the Ridge, and cut our names into endurin'
granite ?"

"I'd forgot that — how come you to remember it ?"

"On account of your havin' lost the chisel
and the tombstone man a-worryin' me about
it to this day. I'll take you to the place.
There's climbin' but it won't hurt us none,
though we ain't as young as we might be.
You says to me, you says: 'Jane, darlin', as
long as them letters stays cut into the ever-
lastin' rock, just so long I'll love you,' you
says, and they's there still."

"Well, I'm here, too, ain't I ?" replied Mr.
Ball, seeming to detect a covert reproach. "I
was allers a great hand fer cuttin'."

"There'll have to be a piece writ in the
end, Ruth, explainin' the happy endin' of the
romance. If you can't do it justice, James and
me can help — James was allers a master hand
at writin'. It'll have to tell how through the
long years he has toiled, hopin' against hope,
and for over thirty years not darin' to write a
line to the object of his affections, not feelin'
worthy, as you may say, and how after her
waitin' faithfully at home and turnin' away
dozens of lovers what pleaded violent-like,

she finally went travellin' in furrin parts and
come upon her old lover a-keepin' a store in a
heathen land, a-strugglin' to retrieve disaster
after disaster at sea, and constantly with-
standin' the blandishments of heathen women
as endeavoured to wean him from his faith,
and how, though very humble and scarcely
darin' to speak, he learned that she was willin'
and they come a sailin' home together and
lived happily ever afterward. Ain't that as
it was, James?"

"Yes'm, except that there wa'n't no particular disaster at sea and them heathen
women did n't exert no blandishments. They
was jest pleasant to an old feller, bless their
little hearts."

By some subtle mental process, Mr. Ball
became aware that he had made a mistake.
"You ain't changed nothin' here, Jane," he
continued, hurriedly, "there's the haircloth
sofy that we used to set on Sunday evenins'
after meetin', and the hair wreath with the
red rose in it made out of my hair and the
white rose made out of your grandmother's
hair on your father's side, and the yeller lily
made out of the hair of your Uncle Jed's
youngest boy. I disremember the rest, but

time was when I could say 'm all. I never see your beat for makin' hair wreaths, Jane. There ain't nothin' gone but the melodeon that used to set by the mantel. What's come of the melodeon?"

"The melodeon is set away in the attic. The mice et out the inside."

"Did n't you hev no cat?"

"There ain't no cat, James, that could get into a melodeon through a mouse hole, more especially the big maltese you gave me. I kept that cat, James, as you may say, all these weary years. When there was kittens, I kept the one that looked most like old Malty, but of late years, the cats has all been different, and the one I buried jest afore I sailed away was yeller and white with black and brown spots — a kinder tortoise shell — that did n't look nothin' like Malty. You'd never have knowed they belonged to the same family, but I was sorry when she died, on account of her bein' the last cat."

Hepsey, half frightened, put her head into the room. "Dinner's ready," she shouted, hurriedly shutting the door.

"Give me your arm, James," said Mrs. Ball, and Ruth followed them into the dining-room.

The retired sailor ate heartily, casting occasional admiring glances at Ruth and Hepsey. It was the innocent approval which age bestows upon youth. "These be the finest biscuit," he said, "that I've had for many a day. I reckon you made 'em, did n't you, young woman?"

"Yes, sir," replied Hepsey, twisting her apron.

The bride was touched in a vulnerable spot.

"Hepsey," she said, decisively, "when your week is up, you will no longer be in my service. I am a-goin' to make a change."

Mr. Ball's knife dropped with a sharp clatter. "Why, Mis' Ball," he said, reproachfully, "who air you goin' to hev to do your work?"

"Don't let that trouble you, James," she answered, serenely, " the washin' can be put out to the Widder Pendleton, her as was Elmiry Peavey, and the rest ain't no particular trouble."

"Aunty," said Ruth, "now that you 've come home and everything is going on nicely, I think I 'd better go back to the city. You see, if I stay here, I 'll be interrupting the honeymoon."

"No, no, Niece Ruth!" exclaimed Mr. Ball, "you ain't interruptin' no honeymoon. It's a great pleasure to your aunt and me to hev you here — we likes pretty young things around us, and as long as we hev a home, you're welcome to stay in it; ain't she Jane?"

"She has sense enough to see, James, that she is interruptin' the honeymoon," replied Aunt Jane, somewhat harshly. "On account of her mother havin' been a Hathaway before marriage, she knows things. Not but what you can come some other time, Ruth," she added, with belated hospitality.

"Thank you, Aunty, I will. I'll stay just a day or two longer, if you don't mind — just until Mr. Winfield comes back. I don't know just where to write to him."

"Mr. — who?" demanded Aunt Jane, looking at her narrowly.

"Mr. Carl Winfield," said Ruth, crimsoning — "the man I am going to marry." The piercing eyes were still fixed upon her.

"Now about the letters, Aunty," she went on, in confusion, "you could help Uncle James with the book much better than I could. Of course it would have to be done under your supervision."

Mrs. Ball scrutinized her niece long and carefully. "You appear to be tellin' the truth," she said. "Who would best print it?"

"I think it would be better for you to handle it yourself, Aunty, and then you and Uncle James would have all the profits. If you let some one else publish it and sell it, you'd have only ten per cent, and even then, you might have to pay part of the expenses."

"How much does it cost to print a book?"

"That depends on the book. Of course it costs more to print a large one than a small one."

"That need n't make no difference," said Aunt Jane, after long deliberation. James has two hundred dollars sewed up on the inside of the belt he insists on wearin', instead of Christian suspenders, ain't you, James?"

"Yes 'm, two hundred and four dollars in my belt and seventy-six cents in my pocket."

"It 's from his store," Mrs. Ball explained. "He sold it to a relative of one of them heathen women."

"It was worth more 'n three hundred," he said regretfully.

"Now, James, you know a small store like that ain't worth no three hundred dollars. I would n't have let you took three hundred, 'cause it would n't be honest."

The arrival of a small and battered trunk created a welcome diversion. "Where's your trunk, Uncle James?" asked Ruth.

"I ain't a needin' of no trunk," he answered, "what clothes I 've got is on me, and that there valise has more of my things in it. When my clothes wears out, I put on new ones and leave tne others for some pore creeter what may need 'em worse 'n me."

Aunt Jane followed Joe upstairs, issuing caution and direction at every step. "You can set outside now, Joe Pendleton," she said, "and see that them hosses don't run away, and as soon as I get some of my things hung up so's they won't wrinkle no more, I 'll come out and pay you."

Joe obeyed, casting longing eyes at a bit of blue gingham that was fluttering among the currant bushes in the garden. Mr. Ball, longing for conversation with his kind, went out to the gate and stood looking up at him, blinking in the bright sunlight.

"Young feller," he said, "I reckon that starboard hoss is my old mare. Where'd you get it?"

"Over to the Ridge," answered Joe, "of a feller named Johnson."

"Jest so — I reckon 't was his father I give Nellie to when I went away. She was a frisky filly then — she don't look nothin' like that now."

"Mamie" turned, as if her former master's voice had stirred some old memory. "She's got the evil eye," Mr. Ball continued. "You wanter be keerful."

"She's all right, I guess," Joe replied.

"Young feller," said Mr. Ball earnestly, "do you chaw terbacker?"

"Yep, but I ain't got no more. I'm on the last hunk."

Mr. Ball stroked his stained beard. "I useter," he said, reminiscently, "afore I was merried."

Joe whistled idly, still watching for Hepsey.

"Young feller," said Mr. Ball, again, "there's a great deal of merryin' and givin' in merriage in this here settlement, ain't there?"

"Not so much as there might be."

"Say, was your mother's name Elmiry Peavey?"

"Yes sir," Joe answered, much surprised.

"Then you be keerful," cautioned Mr. Ball.

"Your hoss has got the evil eye and your father, as might hev been, allers had a weak eye fer women." Joe's face was a picture of blank astonishment.

"I was engaged to both of 'em," Mr. Ball explained, "each one a-keepin' of it secret, and she —" here he pointed his thumb suggestively toward the house — "she's got me."

"I'm going to be married myself," volunteered Joe, proudly.

"Merriage is a fleetin' show — I would n't, if I was in your place. Merriage is a drag on a man's ambitions. I set out to own a schooner, but I can't never do it now, on account of oein' merried. I had a good start towards it — I had a little store all to myself, what was worth three or four hundred dollars, in a sunny country where the women folks had soft voices and pretty ankles and was n't above passin' jokes with an old feller to cheer 'im on 'is lonely way."

Mrs. Ball appeared at the upper window. "James," she called, "you'd better come in and get your hat. Your bald spot will get all sunburned."

"I guess I won't wait no longer, Miss Hathaway," Joe shouted, and, suiting the action to the word, turned around and started down hill. Mr. Ball, half way up the gravelled walk, turned back to smile at Joe with feeble jocularity.

Hearing the familiar voice, Hepsey hastened to the front of the house, and was about to retreat, when Mr. Ball stopped her.

"Pore little darlin', he said, kindly, noting her tear stained face. "Don't go — wait a minute." He fumbled at his belt and at last extracted a crisp, new ten dollar bill. "Here, take that and buy you a ribbon or sunthin' to remember your lovin' Uncle James by."

Hepsey's face brightened, and she hastily concealed the bill in her dress. "I ain't your niece," she said, hesitatingly, "it's Miss Thorne."

"That don't make no difference," rejoined Mr. Ball, generously, "I'm willin' you should be my niece too. All pretty young things is my nieces and I loves 'em all. Won't you give your pore old uncle a kiss to remember you by?"

Ruth, who had heard the last words, came down to the gravelled walk. "Aunt Jane is coming," she announced, and Hepsey fled.

When the lady of the house appeared, Uncle
James was sitting at one end of the piazza
and Ruth at the other, exchanging decorous
commonplaces.

XIII

Plans

HEPSEY had been gone an hour before Mrs. Ball realised that she had sent away one of the witnesses of her approaching wedding. "It don't matter," she said to Ruth, "I guess there's others to be had. I've got the dress and the man and one of 'em and I have faith that the other things will come."

Nevertheless, the prob'em assumed undue proportions. After long study, she decided upon the minister's wife. "If 't wa'nt that the numskulls round here could n't understand two weddin's," she said, "I'd have it in the church, as me and James first planned."

Preparations for the ceremony went forward with Aunt Jane's customary decision and briskness. She made a wedding cake, assisted by Mr. Ball, and gathered all the flowers in the garden. There was something pathetic about her pleasure; it was as though

a wedding had been laid away in lavender, not to see the light for more than thirty
years.

Ruth was to assist in dressing the bride and
then go after the minister and his wife, who,
by Aunt Jane's decree, were to have no previous warning. " 'T ain't necessary to tell
'em beforehand, not as I see," said Mrs. Ball.
" You must ask fust if they 're both to home,
and if only one of 'em is there, you 'll have to
find somebody else. If the minister 's to
home and his wife ain't gaddin', he 'll get
them four dollars in James's belt, leavin' an
even two hundred, or do you think two dollars would be enough for a plain marriage ? "

" I 'd leave that to Uncle James, Aunty."

" I reckon you 're right, Ruth — you 've got
the Hathaway sense."

The old wedding gown was brought down
from the attic and taken out of its winding
sheet. It had been carefully folded, but every
crease showed plainly and parts of it had
changed in colour. Aunt Jane put on her best
"foretop," which was entirely dark, with no
softening grey hair, and was reserved for
occasions of high state. A long brown curl,
which was hers by right of purchase, was

pinned to the hard, uncompromising twist at the back of her neck.

Ruth helped her into the gown and, as it slipped over her head, she inquired, from the depths of it: "Is the front door locked?"

"Yes, Aunty, and the back door too."

"Did you bring up the keys as I told you to?"

"Yes, Aunty, here they are. Why?"

There was a pause, then Mrs. Ball said solemnly: "I've read a great deal about bride-grooms havin' wanderin' fits immediately before weddin's. Does my dress hike up in the back, Ruth?"

It was a little shorter in the back than in the front and cleared the floor on all sides, since she had grown a little after it was made, but Ruth assured her that everything was all right. When they went downstairs together, Mr. Ball was sitting in the parlour, plainly nervous.

"Now Ruth," said Aunt Jane, "you can go after the minister. My first choice is Methodis', after that Baptis' and then Presbyterian. I will entertain James durin' your absence."

Ruth was longing for fresh air and gladly undertook the delicate mission. Before she was half way down the hill, she met Winfield, who had come on the afternoon train.

"You're just in time to see a wedding," she said, when the first raptures had subsided.

"Whose wedding, sweetheart? Ours?"

"Far from it," answered Ruth, laughing. "Come with me and I'll explain."

She gave him a vivid description of the events that had transpired during his absence, and had invited him to the wedding before it occurred to her that Aunt Jane might not be pleased.

"I may be obliged to recall my invitation," she said seriously, "I'll have to ask Aunty about it. She may not want you."

"That doesn't make any difference," announced Winfield, in high spirits, "I'm a-goin' to the wedding and I'm a-goin' to kiss the bride, if you'll let me."

Ruth smothered a laugh. "You may, if you want to, and I won't be jealous. Isn't that sweet of me?"

"You're always sweet, dear. Is this the abode of the parson?"

The Methodist minister was at home, but his wife was not, and Ruth determined to take Winfield in her place. The clergyman said that he would come immediately, and, as the lovers loitered up the hill, they arrived at the same time.

Winfield was presented to the bridal couple, but there was no time for conversation, since Aunt Jane was in a hurry. After the brief ceremony was over, Ruth said wickedly:

"Aunty, on the way to the minister's, Mr. Winfield told me he was going to kiss the bride. I hope you don't mind?"

Winfield looked unutterable things at Ruth, but nobly fulfilled the obligation. Uncle James beamed upon Ruth in a way which indicated that an attractive idea lay behind it, and Winfield created a diversion by tipping over a vase of flowers. "He shan't," he whispered to Ruth, "I'll be darned if he shall!"

"Ruth," said Aunt Jane, after a close scrutiny of Winfield, "if you're layin' out to marry that awkward creeter, what ain't accustomed to a parlour, you'd better do it now, while him and the minister are both here."

Winfield was willing, but Ruth said that one wedding at a time was enough in any family, and the minister, pledged to secrecy, took his departure. The bride cut the wedding cake and each solemnly ate a piece of it. It was a sacrament, rather than a festivity.

When the silence became oppressive, Ruth suggested a walk.

"You will set here, Niece Ruth," remarked Aunt Jane, "until I have changed my dress."

Uncle James sighed softly, as she went upstairs. "Well," he said, "I'm married now, hard and fast, and there ain't no help for it, world without end."

"Cheer up, Uncle," said Winfield, consolingly, "it might be worse."

"It's come on me all of a sudden," he rejoined. "I ain't had no time to prepare for it, as you may say. Little did I think, three weeks ago, as I set in my little store, what was wuth four or five hundred dollars, that before the month was out, I'd be married. Me! Married!" he exclaimed, "Me, as never thought of sech!"

When Mrs. Ball entered, clad in sombre calico, Ruth, overcome by deep emotion, led her lover into the open air. "It's bad for you to stay in there," she said gravely, "when you are destined to meet the same fate."

" I 've had time to prepare for it," he answered, " in fact, I 've had more time than I want."

They wandered down the hillside with aimless leisure, and Ruth stooped to pick up a large, grimy handkerchief, with " C. W." in the corner. " Here 's where we were the other morning," she said.

" Blessed spot," he responded, "beautiful Hepsey and noble Joe ! By what humble means are great destinies made evident ! You have n't said you were glad to see me, dear."

" I 'm always glad to see you, Mr. Winfield," she replied primly.

" Mr. Winfield is n't my name," he objected, taking her into his arms.

" Carl," she whispered shyly, to his coat collar.

" That is n't all of it."

" Carl — dear —" said Ruth, with her face crimson.

" That 's more like it. Now let 's sit down —I 've brought you something and you have three guesses."

" Returned manuscript ? "

" No, you said they were all in."

"Another piece of Aunt Jane's wedding cake ? "

"No, guess again."

" Chocolates ? "

" Who 'd think you were so stupid," he said, putting two fingers into his waistcoat pocket.

" Oh — h ! " gasped Ruth, in delight.

" You funny girl, did n't you expect an engagement ring ?   Let 's see if it fits."

He slipped the gleaming diamond on her finger and it fitted exactly.   "How did you guess ?" she asked, after a little.

" It was n't wholly guess work, dearest." From another pocket, he drew a glove, of grey suede, that belonged to Ruth's left hand.

"Where did you get that ? "

" By the log across the path, that first day, when you were so cross to me."

"I was n't cross ! "

"Yes you were — you were a little fiend."

"Will you forgive me ? " she pleaded, lifting her face to his.

"Rather ! "   He forgave her half a dozen times before she got away from him.   "Now let 's talk sense," she said.

"We can't — I never expect to talk sense again."

"Pretty compliment, is n't it?" she asked.
"It's like your telling me I was brilliant and
then saying I was n't at all like myself."

"Won't you forgive me?" he inquired
significantly.

"Some other time," she said, flushing,
"now what are we going to do?"

"Well," he began, "I saw the oculist, and
he says that my eyes are almost well again,
but that I must n't use them for two weeks
longer. Then, I can read or write for two
hours every day, increasing gradually as long
as they don't hurt. By the first of October,
he thinks I 'll be ready for work again. Carlton wants me to report on the morning of the
fifth, and he offers me a better salary than I
had on *The Herald*."

"That's good!"

"We 'll have to have a flat in the city, or a
little house in the country, near enough for
me to get to the office."

"For us to get to the office," supplemented
Ruth.

"What do you think you 're going to do,
Miss Thorne?"

"Why — I 'm going to keep right on with
the paper," she answered in surprise.

"No you're not, darling," he said, putting his arm around her. "Do you suppose I'm going to have Carlton or any other man giving my wife an assignment? You can't any way, because I've resigned your position for you, and your place is already filled. Carlton sent his congratulations and said his loss was my gain, or something like that. He takes all the credit to himself."

"Why — why — you wretch!"

"I'm not a wretch — you said yourself I was nice. Look here, Ruth," he went on, in a different tone, "what do you think I am? Do you think for a minute that I'd marry you if I couldn't take care of you?"

"'T isn't that," she replied, freeing herself from his encircling arm, "but I like my work and I don't want to give it up. Besides — besides — I thought you'd like to have me near you."

"I do want you near me, sweetheart, that isn't the point. You have the same right that I have to any work that is your natural expression, but, in spite of the advanced age in which we live, I can't help believing that home is the place for a woman. I may be old fashioned, but I don't want my wife

working down town — I 've got too much
pride for that. You have your typewriter,
and you can turn out Sunday specials by the
yard, if you want to. Besides, there are all the
returned manuscripts — if you have the time
and are n't hurried, there 's no reason why
you should nt' do work that they can't afford
to refuse."

Ruth was silent, and he laid his hand upon
hers. "You understand me, don't you, dear?
God knows I 'm not asking you to let your
soul rust out in idleness, and I would n't have
you crave expression that was denied you,
but I don't want you to have to work when
you don't feel like it, nor be at anybody's
beck and call. I know you did good work
on the paper — Carlton spoke of it, too — but
others can do it as well. I want you to do
something that is so thoroughly you that no
one else can do it. It 's a hard life, Ruth, you
know that as well as I do, and I — I love
you."

His last argument was convincing. "I
won't do anything you don't want me to do,
dear," she said, with a new humility.

"I want you to be happy, dearest," he answered, quickly. "Just try my way for a

year — that's all I ask. I know your independence is sweet to you, but the privilege of
working for you with hand and brain, with
your love in my heart; with you at home, to
be proud of me when I succeed and to give
me new courage when I fail, why, it's the
sweetest thing I've ever known."

"I'll have to go back to town very soon,
though," she said, a little later, "I am interrupting the honeymoon."

"We'll have one of our own very soon
that you can't interrupt, and, when you go
back, I'm going with you. We'll buy things
for the house."

"We need lots of things, don't we?" she
asked.

"I expect we do, darling, but I haven't the
least idea what they are. You'll have to tell
me."

"Oriental rugs, for one thing," she said,
"and a mahogany piano, and an instrument
to play it with, because I haven't any parlour
tricks, and some good pictures, and a waffle
iron and a porcelain rolling pin."

"What do you know about rolling pins
and waffle irons?" he asked fondly.

"My dear boy," she replied, patronisingly,

"you forget that in the days when I was a free and independent woman, I was on a newspaper. I know lots of things that are utterly strange to you, because, in all probability, you never ran a woman's department. If you want soup, you must boil meat slowly, and if you want meat, you must boil it rapidly, and if dough sticks to a broom straw when you jab it into a cake, it isn't done."

He laughed joyously. "How about the porcelain rolling pin?"

"It's germ proof," she rejoined, soberly.

"Are we going to keep house on the antiseptic plan?"

"We are — it's better than the installment plan, isn't it? Oh, Carl!" she exclaimed, "I've had the brightest idea!"

"Spring it!" he demanded.

"Why, Aunt Jane's attic is full of old furniture, and I believe she'll give it to us!"

His face fell. "How charming," he said, without emotion.

"Oh, you stupid," she laughed, "it's colonial mahogany, every stick of it! It only needs to be done over!"

"Ruth, you're a genius."

"Wait till I get it, before you praise me.

Just stay here a minute and I'll run up to see what frame of mind she's in."

When she entered the kitchen, the bride was busily engaged in getting supper. Uncle James, with a blue gingham apron tied under his arms, was awkwardly peeling potatoes. "Oh, how good that smells!" exclaimed Ruth, as a spicy sheet of gingerbread was taken out of the oven.

Aunt Jane looked at her kindly, with gratified pride beaming from every feature. "I wish you'd teach me to cook, Aunty," she continued, following up her advantage, "you know I'm going to marry Mr. Winfield."

"Why, yes, I'll teach you — where is he?"

"He's outside — I just came in to speak to you a minute."

"You can ask him to supper if you want to."

"Thank you, Aunty, that's lovely of you. I know he'll like to stay."

"James," said Mrs. Ball, "you're peelin' them pertaters with thick peelins' and you'll land in the poorhouse. I've never knowed it to fail."

"I wanted to ask you something, Aunty," Ruth went on quickly, though feeling that the moment was not auspicious, "you know all that old furniture up in the attic?"

"Well, what of it?"

"Why—why—you are n't using it, you know, and I thought perhaps you 'd be willing to give it to us, so that we can go to house-keeping as soon as we 're married."

"It was your grandmother's," Aunt Jane replied after long thought, "and, as you say, I ain't usin' it. I don't know but what you might as well have it as anybody else. I lay out to buy me a new haircloth parlour suit with that two hundred dollars of James's — he give the minister the hull four dollars over and above that—and—yes, you can have it," she concluded.

Ruth kissed her, with real feeling. "Thank you so much, Aunty. It will be lovely to have something that was my grandmother's."

When she went back to Winfield, he was absorbed in a calculation he was making on the back of an envelope.

"You 're not to use your eyes," she said warningly, "and, oh Carl! It was my grand-mother's and she 's given us every bit of it, and you 're to stay to supper!"

"Must be in a fine humour," he observed.

"I'm ever so glad. Come here, darling, you don't know how I've missed you."

"I've been earning furniture," she said, settling down beside him. "People earn what they get from Aunty—I won't say that, though, because it's mean."

"Tell me about this remarkable furniture. What is it, and how much of it is destined to glorify our humble cottage?"

"It's all ours," she returned serenely, "but I don't know just how much there is. I didn't look at it closely, you know, because I never expected to have any of it. Let's see—there's a heavy dresser, and a large, round table, with claw feet—that's our dining-table, and there's a bed, just like those in the windows in town, when it's done over, and there's a big old-fashioned sofa, and a spinning-wheel—"

"Are you going to spin?"

"Hush, don't interrupt. There are five chairs — dining-room chairs, and two small tables, and a card table with a leaf that you can stand up against the wall, and two lovely rockers, and I don't know what else."

"That's a fairly complete inventory, considering that you 'didn't look at it closely.' What a little humbug you are!"

"You like humbugs, don't you?"

"Some, not all."

There was a long silence, and then Ruth moved away from him. "Tell me about everything," she said. "Think of all the years I haven't known you!"

"There's nothing to tell, dear. Are you going to conduct an excavation into my 'past?'"

"Indeed, I'm not! The present is enough for me, and I'll attend to your future myself."

"There's not much to be ashamed of, Ruth," he said, soberly. "I've always had the woman I should marry in my mind — 'the not impossible she,' and my ideal has kept me out of many a pitfall. I wanted to go to her with clean hands and a clean heart, and I have. I'm not a saint, but I'm as clean as I could be, and live in the world at all."

Ruth put her hand on his. "Tell me about your mother."

A shadow crossed his face and he waited a moment before speaking. "My mother died when I was born," he said with an effort. "I can't tell you about her, Ruth, she — she — wasn't a very good woman."

"Forgive me, dear," she answered with quick sympathy, "I don't want to know!"

"I did n't know about it until a few years ago," he continued, "when some kindly disposed relatives of father's gave me full particulars. They 're dead now, and I 'm glad of it. She — she — drank."

"Don't, Carl!" she cried, "I don't want to know!"

"You 're a sweet girl, Ruth," he said, tenderly, touching her hand to his lips. "Father died when I was ten or twelve years old and I can't remember him very well, though I have one picture, taken a little while before he was married. He was a moody, silent man, who hardly ever spoke to any one. I know now that he was broken-hearted. I can't remember even the tones of his voice, but only one or two little peculiarities. He could n't bear the smell of lavender and the sight of any shade of purple actually made him suffer. It was very strange.

"I 've picked up what education I have," he went on. "I have nothing to give you, Ruth, but these —" he held out his hands — "and my heart."

"That 's all I want, dearest — don't tell me any more!"

A bell rang cheerily, and, when they went

in, Aunt Jane welcomed him with apparent
cordiality, though a close observer might have
detected a tinge of suspicion. She liked the
ring on Ruth's finger, which she noticed for
the first time. "It's real pretty, ain't it,
James?" she asked.

"Yes'm, 'tis so."

"It's just come to my mind now that you
never give me no ring except this here one
we was married with. I guess we'd better
take some of that two hundred dollars you've
got sewed up in that unchristian belt you
insist on wearin' and get me a ring like Ruth's,
and use the rest for furniture, don't you think
so?"

"Yes'm," he replied. "Ring and furniture — or anythin' you'd like."

"James is real indulgent," she said to Winfield, with a certain modest pride which was
at once ludicrous and pathetic.

"He should be, Mrs. Ball," returned the
young man, gallantly.

She looked at him closely, as if to discover
whether he was in earnest, but he did not
flinch. "Young feller," she said, "you ain't
layin' out to take no excursions on the water,
be you?"

"Not that I know of," he answered, "why?"

" Sea-farin' is dangerous," she returned.

" Mis' Ball was terrible sea sick comin' here," remarked her husband. "She did n't seem to have no sea legs, as you may say."

"Ain't you tired of dwellin' on that?" asked Aunt Jane, sharply. "'T ain't no disgrace to be sea sick, and I wan't the only one."

Winfield came to the rescue with a question and the troubled waters were soon calm again. After supper, Ruth said: "Aunty, may I take Mr. Winfield up to the attic and show him my grandmother's things that you 've just given me?"

"Run along, child. Me and James will wash the dishes."

" Poor James," said Winfield, in a low tone, as they ascended the stairs. "Do I have to wash dishes, Ruth?"

" It would n't surprise me. You sai⅃ you wanted to work for me, and I despise dishes."

" Then we 'll get an orphan to do 'em. I 'm not fitted for it, and I don't think you are.

"Say, is n't this great!" he exclaimed, as they entered the attic. "Trunks, cobwebs, and old furniture! Why have I never been here before?"

"It was n't proper," replied Ruth, primly, with a sidelong glance at him. "No, go away!"

They dragged the furniture out into the middle of the room and looked it over critically. There was all that she had described, and unsuspected treasure lay in concealment behind it. "There's almost enough to furnish a flat!" she cried, in delight.

He was opening the drawers of a cabinet, which stood far back under the eaves. "What's this, Ruth?"

"Oh, it's old blue china—willow pattern! How rich we are!"

"Is old blue willow-pattern china considered beautiful?"

"Of course it is, you goose! We'll have to have our dining-room done in old blue, now, with a shelf on the wall for these plates."

"Why can't we have a red dining-room?"

"Because it would be a fright. You can have a red den, if you like."

"All right," he answered, "but it seems to me it would be simpler and save a good deal of expense, if we just pitched the plates into the sad sea. I don't think much of 'em."

"That's because you're not educated

dearest," returned Ruth, sweetly. "When you're married, you'll know a great deal more about china—you see if you don't."

They lingered until it was so dark that they could scarcely see each other's faces. "We'll come up again to-morrow," she said. "Wait a minute."

She groped over to the east window, where there was still a faint glow, and lighted the lamp, which stood in its accustomed place, newly filled.

"You're not going to leave it burning, are you?" he asked.

"Yes, Aunt Jane has a light in this window every night."

"Why, what for?"

"I don't know, dearest. I think it's for a lighthouse, but I don't care. Come, let's go downstairs."

XIV

"For Remembrance"

THE next day, while Ruth was busily gathering up her few belongings and packing her trunk, Winfield appeared with a suggestion regarding the advisability of outdoor exercise. Uncle James stood at the gate and watched them as they went down hill. He was a pathetic old figure, predestined to loneliness under all circumstances.

"That's the way I'll look when we've been married a few years," said Carl.

"Worse than that," returned Ruth, gravely. "I'm sorry for you, even now."

"You need n't be proud and haughty just because you've had a wedding at your house —we're going to have one at ours."

"At ours?"

"At the 'Widder's,' I mean, this very evening."

"That's nice," answered Ruth, refusing to ask the question.

199

"It's Joe and Hepsey," he continued, "and I thought perhaps you might stoop low enough to assist me in selecting an appropriate wedding gift in yonder seething mart. I feel greatly indebted to them."

"Why, of course I will; it's quite sudden, is n't it?"

"Far be it from me to say so. However, it's the most reversed wedding I ever heard of. A marriage at the home of the groom, to say the least, is unusual. Moreover, the 'Widder' Pendleton is to take the bridal tour and leave the happy couple at home. She's going to visit a relative who is distant in both position and relationship—all unknown to the relative, I fancy. She starts immediately after the ceremony and it seems to me that it would be a pious notion to throw rice and old shoes after her."

"Why, Carl! You don't want to maim her, do you?"

"I would n't mind. If it had n't been for my ostrich-like digestion, I would n't have had anything to worry about by this time. However, if you insist, I will throw the rice and let you heave the shoes. If you have the precision of aim which distinguishes your sex, the 'Widder' will escape uninjured."

"Am I to be invited?"

"Certainly—have n't I already invited you?"

"They may not like it."

"That does n't make any difference. Lots of people go to weddings who are n't wanted."

"I 'll go, then," announced Ruth, "and once again, I give you my gracious permission to kiss the bride."

"Thank you, dear, but I 'm not going to kiss any brides except my own. I 've signed the pledge and sworn off."

They created a sensati in the village when they acquired the set of china which had been on exhibition over a year. During that time it had fallen at least a third in price, though its value was unchanged. Ruth bought a hideous red table-cloth, which she knew would please Hepsey, greatly to Winfield's disgust.

"Why do you do that?" he demanded. "Don 't you know that, in all probability, I 'll have to eat off of it? I much prefer the oil-cloth, to which I am now accustomed."

"You 'll have to get used to table linen,

dear," she returned teasingly; "it's my ambition to have one just like this for state occasions."

Joe appeared with the chariot just in time to receive and transport the gift. "Here's your wedding present, Joe!" called Winfield, and the innocent villagers formed a circle about them as the groom-elect endeavoured to express his appreciation. Winfield helped him pack the "101 pieces" on the back seat and under it, and when Ruth, feeling like a fairy godmother, presented the red table-cloth, his cup of joy was full.

He started off proudly, with a soup tureen and two platters on the seat beside him. The red table-cloth was slung over his arm, in toreador fashion, and the normal creak of the conveyance was accentuated by an ominous rattle of crockery. Then he circled back, motioning them to wait.

"Here's sunthin' I most forgot," he said, giving Ruth a note. "I'd drive you back fer nothin', only I've got sech a load."

The note was from Miss Ainslie, inviting Miss Thorne and her friend to come at five o'clock and stay to tea. No answer was expected unless she could not come.

The quaint, old-fashioned script was in some way familiar. A flash of memory took Ruth back to the note she had found in the dresser drawer, beginning: "I thank you from my heart for understanding me." So it was Miss Ainslie who had sent the mysterious message to Aunt Jane.

"You're not paying any attention to me," complained Winfield. "I suppose, when we're married, I'll have to write out what I want to say to you, and put it on file."

"You're a goose," laughed Ruth. "We're going to Miss Ainslie's to-night for tea. Aren't we getting gay?"

"Indeed we are! Weddings and teas follow one another like Regret on the heels of Pleasure."

"Pretty simile," commented Ruth. "If we go to the tea, we'll have to miss the wedding."

"Well, we've been to a wedding quite recently, so I suppose it's better to go to the tea. Perhaps, by arranging it, we might be given nourishment at both places — not that I pine for the 'Widder's' cooking. Anyhow, we've sent our gift, and they'd rather have that than to have us, if they were permitted to choose."

"Do you suppose they 'll give us anything?"

"Let us hope not."

"I don't believe we want any at all," she said. "Most of them would be in bad taste, and you 'd have to bury them at night, one at a time, while I held a lantern."

"The policeman on the beat would come and ask us what we were doing," he objected; "and when we told him we were only burying our wedding presents, he would n't believe us. We 'd be dragged to the station and put into a noisome cell. Would n't it make a pretty story for the morning papers! The people who gave us the things would enjoy it over their coffee."

"It would be pathetic, would n't it?"

"It would, Miss Thorne. I think we 'd better not tell anybody until its all safely over, and then we can have a little card printed to go with the announcement, saying that if anybody is inclined to give us a present, we 'd rather have the money."

"You 're a very practical person, Carl. One would think you had been married several times."

"We 'll be married as often as you like,

dear. Judging by your respected aunt, one ceremony is n't 'rightfully bindin', and I want it done often enough to be sure that you can't get away from me."

As they entered the gate, Uncle James approached stealthily by a roundabout way and beckoned to them. "Excuse me," he began, as they came within speaking distance, "but has Mis' Ball give you furniture?"

"Yes," replied Ruth, in astonishment, "why?"

"There's clouds to starboard and she's repentin'. She's been admirin' of it the hull mornin' in the attic. I was sot in the kitchen with pertaters," he explained, "but the work is wearin' and a feller needs fresh air."

"Thank you for the tip, Uncle,' said Winfield, heartily.

The old man glowed with gratification. "We men understand each other," was plainly written on his expressive face, as he went noiselessly back to the kitchen.

"You'd better go home, dear," suggested Ruth.

"Delicate hint," replied Winfield. "It would take a social strategist to perceive your hidden meaning. Still, my finer sensibilities respond instantly to your touch, and I will go. I flatter myself that I've never had to be put out yet, when I've been calling on a girl. Some subtle suggestion like yours has always been sufficient."

"Don't be cross, dear—let's see how soon you can get to the bottom of the hill. You can come back at four o'clock."

He laughed and turned back to wave his hand at her. She wafted a kiss from the tips of her fingers, which seemed momentarily to impede his progress, but she motioned him away and ran into the house.

Aunt Jane was nowhere to be seen, so she went on into the kitchen to help Uncle James with the potatoes. He had peeled almost a peck and the thick parings lay in a heap on the floor. "My goodness!" she exclaimed. "You'd better throw those out, Uncle, and I'll put the potatoes on to boil."

He hastened out, with his arms full of peelings. "You're a real kind woman, Niece Ruth," he said gratefully, when he came in. "You don't favour your aunt none—I think you're more like me."

Mrs. Ball entered the kitchen with a cloud upon her brow, and in one of those rare flashes of insight which are vouchsafed to plodding mortals, a plan of action presented itself to Ruth.

"Aunty," she said, before Mrs. Ball had time to speak, "you know I'm going back to the city to-morrow, and I'd like to send you and Uncle James a wedding present — you've been so good to me. What shall it be?"

"Well, now, I don't know," she answered, visibly softening, "but I'll think it over, and let you know."

"What would you like, Uncle James?"

"You needn't trouble him about it," explained his wife. "He'll like whatever I do, won't you, James?"

"Yes'm, just as you say."

After dinner, when Ruth broached the subject of furniture, she was gratified to find that Aunt Jane had no serious objections. "I kinder hate to part with it, Ruth," she said, "but in a way, as you may say, it's yours."

"'T isn't like giving it away, Aunty — it's all in the family, and, as you say, you're not using it."

"That's so, and then James and me are likely to come and make you a long visit, so I'll get the good of it, too."

Ruth was momentarily stunned, but rallied enough to express great pleasure at the prospect. As Aunt Jane began to clear up the dishes, Mr. Ball looked at his niece, with a certain quiet joy, and then, unmistakably, winked.

"When you decide about the wedding present, Aunty, let me know, won't you?" she asked, as Mrs. Ball came in after the rest of the dishes. "Mr. Winfield would like to send you a remembrance also." Then Ruth added, to her conscience, "I know he would."

"He seems like a pleasant-spoken feller," remarked Aunt Jane. "You can ask him to supper to-night, if you like."

"Thank you, Aunty, but we're going to Miss Ainslie's."

"Huh!" snorted Mrs. Ball. "Mary Ainslie ain't got no sperrit!" With this enigmatical statement, she sailed majestically out of the room.

During the afternoon, Ruth finished her packing, leaving out a white shirt-waist to wear to Miss Ainslie's. When she went down to the parlour to wait for Winfield, Aunt Jane appeared, with her husband in her wake.

"Ruth," she announced, "me and James

have decided on a weddin' present. I would like a fine linen table-cloth and a dozen napkins."

"All right, Aunty."

"And if Mr. Winfield is disposed to it, he can give me a lemonade set — one of them what has different coloured tumblers belongin' to it."

"He'll be pleased to send it, Aunty; I know he will."

"I'm a-layin' out to take part of them two hundred dollars what's sewed up in James's belt, and buy me a new black silk," she went on. "I've got some real lace to trim it with, what James give me in the early years of our engagement. Don't you think a black silk is allers nice, Ruth?"

"Yes, it is, Aunty; and just now, it's very stylish."

"You appear to know about such things. I guess I'll let you get it for me in the city when you buy the weddin' present. I'll give you the money, and you can get the linin's too, while you're about it."

"I'll send you some samples, Aunty, and then you can take your choice."

"And—" began Mrs. Ball.

"Did you know Mrs. Pendleton was going away, Aunty?" asked Ruth, hastily.

"Do tell! Elmiry Peavey goin' travellin'?"

"Yes, she's going somewhere for a visit— I don't know just where."

"I had laid out to take James and call on Elmiry," she said, stroking her apron thoughtfully, while a shadow crossed Mr. Ball's expressive face; "but I guess I'll wait now till I get my new black silk. I want her to know I've done well."

A warning hiss from the kitchen and the odour of burning sugar impelled Aunt Jane to a hasty exit just as Winfield came. Uncle James followed them to the door.

"Niece Ruth," he said, hesitating and fumbling at his belt, "be you goin' to get m rried?"

"I hope so, Uncle," she replied kindly.

"Then—then—I wish you'd take this and buy you sunthin' to remember your pore old Uncle James by." He thrust a trembling hand toward her, and offered her a twenty dollar bill.

"Why, Uncle!" she exclaimed. "I mustn't take this! Thank you ever so much, but it isn't right!"

"I'd be pleased," he said plaintively.
"'Taint as if I wan't accustomed to money.
My store was wuth five or six hundred dollars, and you've been real pleasant to me,
Niece Ruth. Buy a hair wreath for the parlour, or sunthin' to remind you of your pore
old Uncle."

Winfield pressed her arm warningly, and
she tucked the bill into her chatelaine bag.
"Thank you, Uncle!" she said; then, of her
own accord, she stooped and kissed him
lightly on the cheek.

A mist came into the old man's eyes, and
he put his hand to his belt again, but she hurriedly led Winfield away. "Ruth," he said,
as they went down the hill, "you're a sweet
girl. That was real womanly kindness to the
poor devil."

"Shall I be equally kind to all 'poor
devils'?"

"There's one more who needs you — if
you attend to him properly, it will be
enough."

"I don't see how they're going to get
Aunty's silk gown and a ring like mine and a
haircloth parlour suit and publish a book with
less than two hundred dollars, do you?"

"Hardly — Joe says that he gave Hepsey ten dollars.   There's a great discussion about the spending of it."

" I did n't know — I feel guilty."

" You need n't, darling.   There was nothing else for you to do.   How did you succeed with your delicate mission ?"

"I managed it," she said proudly.   " I feel that I was originally destined for a diplomatic career."   He laughed when she described the lemonade set which she had promised in his name.

" I 'll see that the furniture is shipped to-morrow," he assured her; " and then I 'll go on a still hunt for the gaudy glassware.   I 'm blessed if I don't give 'em a silver ice pitcher, too."

" I 'm in for a table-cloth and a dozen nap-kins," laughed Ruth; " but I don't mind. We won't bury Uncle's wedding present, will we ?"

"I should say not !   Behold the effect of the card, long before it 's printed."

"I know," said Ruth, seriously, " I 'll get a silver spoon or something like that out of the twenty dollars, and then I 'll spend the rest of it on something nice for Uncle James.   The poor soul is n't getting any wedding present, and he 'll never know."

" There 's a moral question involved in that," replied Winfield. " Is it right to use his money in that way and assume the credit yourself ? "

"We 'll have to think it over," Ruth answered. " It is n't so very simple after all."

Miss Ainslie was waiting for them in the garden and came to the gate to meet them. She wore a gown of lavender taffeta, which rustled and shone in the sunlight. The skirt was slightly trained, with a dust ruffle underneath, and the waist was made in surplice fashion, open at the throat. A bertha of rarest Brussels lace was fastened at her neck with the amethyst pin, inlaid with gold and surrounded by baroque pearls. The ends of the bertha hung loosely and under it she had tied an apron of sheerest linen, edged with narrow Duchesse lace. Her hair was coiled softly on top of her head, with a string of amethysts and another of pearls woven among the silvery strands.

" Welcome to my house," she said, smiling, Winfield at once became her slave. She talked easily, with that exquisite cadence which makes each word seem like a gift, but there was a certain subtle excitement in her manner, which Ruth did not fail to perceive. When Winfield was not looking at Miss Ainslie, her eyes rested upon him with a wondering hunger, mingled with tenderness and fear.

Midsummer lay upon the garden and the faint odour of mignonette and lavender came with every wandering wind. White butterflies and thistledown floated in the air, bees hummed drowsily, and the stately hollyhocks swayed slowly back and forth.

"Do you know why I asked you to come to-day?" She spoke to Ruth, but looked at Winfield.

"Why, Miss Ainslie?"

"Because it is my birthday — I am fifty-five years old."

Ruth's face mirrored her astonishment. "You don't look any older than I do," she said.

Except for the white hair, it was true. Her face was as fresh as a rose with the morning dew upon it, and even on her neck, where the folds of lace revealed a dazzling whiteness, there were no lines.

"Teach us how to live, Miss Ainslie," said

Winfield, softly, "that the end of half a century may find us young."

A delicate pink suffused her cheeks and she turned her eyes to his. "I 've just been happy, that 's all," she answered.

"It needs the alchemist's touch," he said, "to change our sordid world to gold."

"We can all learn," she replied, "and even if we don't try, it comes to us once."

"What ?" asked Ruth.

"Happiness — even if it is n't until the end. In every life there is a perfect moment, like a flash of sun. We can shape our days by that, if we will — before by faith, and afterward by memory."

The conversation drifted to less serious things. Ruth, remembering that Miss Ainslie did not hear the village gossip, described her aunt's home-coming, the dismissal of Hepsey, and told her of the wedding which was to take place that evening. Winfield was delighted, for he had never heard her talk so well, but Miss Ainslie listened with gentle displeasure.

"I did not think Miss Hathaway would ever be married abroad," she said. "I think she should have waited until she came home.

It would have been more delicate to let him follow her. To seem to pursue a gentleman, however innocent one may be, is — is unmaidenly."

Winfield choked, then coughed violently.

"Understand me, dear," Miss Ainslie went on, "I do not mean to criticise your aunt — she is one of my dearest friends. Perhaps I should not have spoken at all," she concluded in genuine distress.

"It's all right, Miss Ainslie," Ruth assured her, "I know just how you feel."

Winfield, having recovered his composure, asked a question about the garden, and Miss Ainslie led them in triumph around her domain. She gathered a little nosegay of sweet-williams for Ruth, who was over among the hollyhocks, then she said shyly: "What shall I pick for you?"

"Anything you like, Miss Ainslie. I am at a loss to choose."

She bent over and plucked a leaf of rosemary, looking at him long and searchingly as she put it into his hand.

"For remembrance," she said, with the deep fire burning in her eyes. Then she added, with a pitiful hunger in her voice:

"Whatever happens, you won't forget me?"

"Never!" he answered, strangely stirred.

"Thank you," she whispered brokenly, drawing away from him. "You look so much like—like some one I used to know."

At dusk they went into the house. Except for the hall, it was square, with two partitions dividing it. The two front rooms were separated by an arch, and the dining-room and kitchen were similarly situated at the back of the house, with a china closet and pantry between them.

Miss Ainslie's table, of solid mahogany, was covered only with fine linen doilies, after a modern fashion, and two quaint candlesticks, of solid silver, stood opposite each other. In the centre, in a silver vase of foreign pattern, there was a great bunch of asters—white and pink and blue.

The repast was simple—chicken fried to a golden brown, with creamed potatoes, a salad made of fresh vegetables from the garden, hot biscuits, deliciously light, and the fragrant Chinese tea, served in the Royal Kaga cups, followed by pound cake, and pears preserved in a heavy red syrup.

The hostess sat at the head of the table, dispensing a graceful hospitality. She made no apology, such as prefaced almost every meal at Aunt Jane's. It was her best, and she was proud to give it — such was the impression.

Afterward, when Ruth told her that she was going back to the city, Miss Ainslie's face grew sad.

"Why — why must you go?" she asked.

"I'm interrupting the honeymoon," Ruth answered, "and when I suggested departure, Aunty agreed to it immediately. I can't very well stay now, can I?"

"My dear," said Miss Ainslie, laying her hand upon Ruth's, "if you could, if you only would—won't you come and stay with me?"

"I'd love to," replied Ruth, impetuously, "but are you sure you want me?"

"Believe me, my dear," said Miss Ainslie, simply, "it will give me great happiness."

So it was arranged that the next day Ruth's trunk should be taken to Miss Ainslie's, and that she would stay until the first of October. Winfield was delighted, since it brought Ruth nearer to him and involved no long separation.

They went outdoors again, where the crickets and katydids were chirping in the grass, and the drowsy twitter of birds came from the maples above. The moon, at its full, swung slowly over the hill, and threads of silver light came into the fragrant dusk of the garden. Now and then the moonlight shone full upon Miss Ainslie's face, touching her hair as if with loving tenderness and giving her an unearthly beauty. It was the face of a saint.

Winfield, speaking reverently, told her of their betrothal. She leaned forward, into the light, and put one hand caressingly upon the arm of each.

"I am so glad," she said, with her face illumined. Through the music of her voice ran lights and shadows, vague, womanly appeal, and a haunting sweetness neither could ever forget.

That night, the gates of Youth turned on their silent hinges for Miss Ainslie. Forgetting the hoary frost that the years had laid upon her hair, she walked, hand in hand with them, through the clover fields which lay fair before them and by the silvered reaches of the River of Dreams. Into their love came something sweet that they had not found before — the absolute need of sharing life together, whether it should be joy or pain. Unknowingly, they rose to that height which makes sacrifice the soul's dearest offering, as the chrysalis, brown and unbeautiful, gives the radiant creature within to the light and freedom of day.

When the whistle sounded for the ten o'clock train, Ruth said it was late and they must go. Miss Ainslie went to the gate with them, her lavender scented gown rustling softly as she walked, and the moonlight making new beauty of the amethysts and pearls entwined in her hair.

Ruth, aglow with happiness, put her arms around Miss Ainslie's neck and kissed her tenderly.

"May I, too?" asked Winfield.

He drew her toward him, without waiting for an answer, and Miss Ainslie trembled from head to foot as she lifted her face to his.

Across the way the wedding was in full blast, but neither of them cared to go. Ruth turned back for a last glimpse of the garden and its gentle mistress, but she was gone, and the light from her candle streamed out until it rested upon a white hollyhock, nodding drowsily.

To Ruth, walking in the starlight with her lover, it seemed as if the world had been made new. The spell was upon Winfield for a long time, but at last he spoke.

" If I could have chosen my mother," he said, simply, " she would have been like Miss Ainslie."

XV

The Secret and the Dream

RUTH easily became accustomed to the quiet life at Miss Ainslie's, and gradually lost all desire to go back to the city. "You're spoiling me," she said, one day. "I don't want to go back to town, I don't want to work, I don't want to do anything but sit still and look at you. I did n't know I was so lazy."

"You're not lazy, dear," answered Miss Ainslie, "you were tired, and you did n't know how tired you were."

Winfield practically lived there. In the morning, he sat in the garden, reading the paper, while Ruth helped about the house. She insisted upon learning to cook, and he ate many an unfamiliar dish, heroically proclaiming that it was good. "You must never doubt his love," Miss Ainslie said, "for those biscuits—well, dear, you know they were—were not just right."

The amateur cook laughed outright at the
gentle criticism. "They were awful," she
admitted, "but I'm going to keep at it until
I learn how."

The upper part of the house was divided
into four rooms, with windows on all sides.
One of the front rooms, with north and east
windows, was Miss Ainslie's, while the one
just back of it, with south and east windows,
was a sitting-room.

"I keep my prettiest things up here, dear,"
she explained to Ruth, "for I don't want
people to think I'm crazy." Ruth caught her
breath as she entered the room, for rare tapes-
tries hung on the walls and priceless rugs
lay on the floor. The furniture, like that
downstairs, was colonial mahogany, highly
polished, with here and there a chair or table
of foreign workmanship. There was a cabinet, filled with rare china, a marquetry table,
and a chair of teakwood, inlaid with mother
of pearl. In one corner of the room was a
large chest of sandal wood, inlaid with pearl
and partly covered by a wonderful antique rug.

The world had seemingly given up its
beauty to adorn Miss Ainslie's room. She had
pottery from Mexico, China and Japan;

strange things from Egypt and the Nile, and
all the Oriental splendour of India and Persia.
Ruth wisely asked no questions, but once, as
before, she said hesitating; "they were given
to me by a—a friend."

After much pleading on Ruth's part, Winfield was allowed to come to the sitting
room. "He'll think I'm silly, dear," she
said, flushing ; but, on the contrary, he shared
Ruth's delight, and won Miss Ainslie's grati-
tude by his appreciation of her treasures.

Day by day, the singular attraction grew
between them. She loved Ruth, but she took
him unreservedly into her heart. Ruth observed, idly, that she never called him "Mr.
Winfield." At first she spoke of him as
"your friend" and afterward, when he had
asked her to, she yielded, with an adorable
shyness, and called him Carl.

He, too, had eaten of the lotus and lost the
desire to go back to town. From the hilltop
they could see the yellow fields and hear the
soft melody of reaping from the valley around
them. He and Ruth often walked together,
but Miss Ainslie never would go with them.
She stayed quietly at home, as she had done
for many years.

Everynight, whenthe last train came from the city, she put a lighted candle in her front window, using always the candlestick of solid silver, covered with fretwork in intricate design. If Winfield was there, she managed to have him and Ruth in another room. At half-past ten, she took it away, sighing softly as she put out the light.

Ruth wondered, but said nothing, even to Winfield. The grain in the valley was bound in sheaves, and the first colour came on the maples—sometimes in a delicate flush, or a flash of gold, and sometimes like a blood-red wound.

One morning, when Miss Ainslie came downstairs, Ruth was startled at the change in her. The quick, light step was slow and heavy, the broad, straight shoulders drooped a little, and her face, while still dimpled and fair, was subtly different. Behind her deep, violet eyes lay an unspeakable sadness and the rosy tints were gone. Her face was as pure and cold as marble, with the peace of the dead laid upon it. She seemed to have grown old in a single night.

All day she said little or nothing and would not eat. She simply sat still, looking out of the east window. "No, she said, gently, to Ruth, "nothing is the matter, deary, I'm just tired."

When Winfield came, she kept him away from Miss Ainslie without seeming to do so. "Let's go for a walk," she said. She tried to speak lightly, but there was a lump in her throat and a tightening at her heart.

They climbed the hill and took the side path which led to the woods, following it down and through the aisles of trees, to the log across the path. Ruth was troubled and sat there some little time without speaking, then suddenly, she knew that something was wrong with Carl.

Her heart was filled with strange foreboding and she vainly tried to swallow the persistent lump in her throat. She spoke to him, gently, once or twice and he did not seem to hear. "Carl!" she cried in agony, "Carl! What is it?"

He tried to shake off the spell which lay upon him. "Nothing, darling," he said unsteadily, with something of the old tenderness. "I'm weak — and foolish — that's all."

"Carl! Dearest!" she cried, and then broke down, sobbing bitterly.

Her tears aroused him and he tried to soothe her. "Ruth, my darling girl, don't cry. We have each other, sweetheart, and it doesn't matter—nothing matters in the whole, wide world."

After a little, she regained her self-control.

"Come out into the sun," he said, "it's ghostly here. You don't seem real to me, Ruth."

The mist filled her eyes again. "Don't, darling," he pleaded, "I'll try to tell you."

They sat down on the hillside, where the sun shone brightly, and where they could see Miss Ainslie's house plainly. She waited, frightened and suffering, for what seemed an eternity, before he spoke.

"Last night, Ruth," he began, "my father came to me in a dream. You know he died when I was about twelve years old, and last night I saw him as he would have been if he had lived until now — something over sixty. His hair and beard were matted and there was the most awful expression in his eyes — it makes me shudder yet. He was in his grave clothes, dead and yet not dead. He was suffering — there was something he was trying to say to me; something he wanted to explain. We were out here on the hill in the moonlight and I could see Miss Ainslie's house and hear the surf behind the cliff. All he could say to me was: 'Abby — Mary — Mary — Abby — she — Mary,' over and over again. Once he said 'mother.' Abby was my mother's name.

"It is terrible," he went on. "I can't understand it. There is something I must do, and I don't know what it is. A command is laid on me by the dead—there is some wrong for which I must atone. When I first awoke, I thought it was a dream, but it is n't, it 's real. It seems as though that was the real world, and this—all our love and happiness, and you, were just dreams. I can't bear it, Ruth!"

He shuddered, and she tried to comfort him, though she was cold as a marble statue and her lips moved with difficulty. "Don't, dear," she said, "it was only a dream. I 've had them sometimes, so vividly that they haunted me for days and, as you say, it seemed as if that was the real world and this the dream. I know how you feel — those things are n't pleasant, but there 's nothing we can do. It makes one feel so helpless. The affairs of the day are largely under our control, but at night, when the body is asleep, the

mind harks back to things that have been forgotten for years. It takes a fevered fancy as
a fact, and builds upon it a whole series of
disasters. It gives trivial things great signifi-
cance and turns life upside down. Remembering it is the worst of all."

"There's something I can't get at, Ruth,"
he answered. "It's just out of my reach. I
know it's reasonable to suppose it was a
dream and that it can be explained by natural
causes, but I don't dream very often."

"I dream every night," she said. "Sometimes they're just silly, foolish things and
sometimes they're vivid and horrible realities
that I can't forget for weeks. But, surely,
dear, we're not foolish enough to believe in
dreams?"

"No, I hope not," he replied, doubtfully.

"Let's go for a little walk," she said, "and
we'll forget it."

Then she told him how changed Miss Ainslie was and how she had left her, sitting aimlessly by the window. "I don't think I'd
better stay away long," she concluded, "she
may need me."

"I won't be selfish, Ruth; we'll go back
now. "I'm sorry Miss Ainslie isn't well."

"She said she was 'just tired' but it is n't
like her to be tired. She does n't seem to
want anybody near her, but you can sit in
the garden this afternoon, if you 'd like to,
and I 'll flit in and out like an industrious butterfly. Some new books have just come, and
I 'll leave them in the arbour for you."

"All right, dear, and if there 's anything I
can do, I hope you 'll tell me."

As they approached the house, a brisk little
man hurried out of the gate and went toward
the village.

"Who 's that?" asked Winfield.

"I don't know—some one who has
brought something, probably. I trust she 's
better."

Miss Ainslie seemed more like herself, as
she moved about the house, dusting and putting the rooms in order, as was her wont.
At noon she fried a bit of chicken for Ruth,
but took nothing herself except a cup of tea.

"No, deary," she said, in answer to Ruth's
anxious question, "I 'm all right—don't fret
about me."

"Have you any pain, Miss Ainslie?"

"No, of course I have n't, you foolish
child!"

She tried to smile, but her white lips quivered pitifully.

In the afternoon, when she said she was cold, Ruth made a fire in the open fireplace, and wheeled Miss Ainslie's favourite chair in front of it. She drew her shawl about her shoulders and leaned back.

"I'm so comfortable, now, she said drowsily; "I think I'm going to sleep, dear."

Ruth sat by her, pretending to read, but, in reality, watching her closely, until the deep, regular breathing assured her that she was asleep. She went out into the garden and found Winfield in the arbour.

"How's this patient?" she asked, kissing him lightly on the forehead.

"I'm all right, dearest," he answered, drawing her down beside him, "and I'm ashamed of myself because I was so foolish."

During the afternoon Ruth made frequent trips to the house, each time finding Miss Ainslie sound asleep. It was after six o'clock when she woke and rubbed her eyes, wonderingly.

"How long have I been asleep, Ruth?"

"All the afternoon, Miss Ainslie — do you feel better now?"

"Yes, I think I do. I did n't sleep last night, but it 's been years since I 've taken a nap in the daytime."

Ruth invited Carl to supper, and made them both sit still while she prepared the simple meal, which, as he said, was "astonishingly good." He was quite himself again, but Miss Ainslie, though trying to assume her old manner, had undergone a great change.

Carl helped Ruth with the dishes, saying he supposed he might as well become accustomed to it, and, feeling the need of sleep, went home very early.

"I 'm all right," he said to Ruth, as he kissed her at the door, "and you 're just the sweetest girl in the world. Good night, darling."

A chill mist came inland, and Ruth kept pine knots burning in the fireplace. They sat without other light, Miss Ainslie with her head resting upon her hand, and Ruth watching her narrowly. Now and then they spoke aimlessly, of commonplaces.

When the last train came in, Miss Ainslie raised her eyes to the silver candlestick that stood on the mantel and sighed.

"Shall I put the light in the window?" asked Ruth.

It was a long time before Miss Ainslie answered.

"No, deary," she said sadly, "never any more."

She was trying to hide her suffering, and Ruth's heart ached for her in vain. The sound of the train died away in the distance and the firelight faded.

"Ruth," she said, in a low voice, "I am going away."

"Away, Miss Ainslie? Where?"

"I don't know, dear — it's where we all go — 'the undiscovered country from whose bourne no traveller returns.' Sometimes it's a long journey and sometimes a short one, but we all take it — alone — at the last."

Ruth's heart throbbed violently, then stood still.

"Don't!" she cried, sharply.

"I'm not afraid, dear, and I'm ready to go, even though you have made me so happy — you and he."

Miss Ainslie waited a moment, then continued, in a different tone :

"To-day the lawyer came and made my will. I haven't much — just this little house, a small income paid semi-annually, and my—

my things. All my things are for you — the house and the income are for — for him."

Ruth was crying softly and Miss Ainslie went to her, laying her hand caressingly upon the bowed head. "Don't, deary," she pleaded, "don't be unhappy. I'm not afraid. I'm just going to sleep, that's all, to wake in immortal dawn. I want you and him to have my things, because I love you—because I've always loved you, and because I will—even afterward."

Ruth choked down her sobs, and Miss Ainslie drew her chair closer, taking the girl's cold hand in hers. That touch, so strong and gentle, that had always brought balm to her troubled spirit, did not fail in its ministry now.

"He went away," said Miss Ainslie, after a long silence, as if in continuation of something she had said before, "and I was afraid. He had made many voyages in safety, each one more successful than the last, and he always brought me beautiful things, but, this time, I knew that it was not right for him to go."

"When he came back, we were to be married." The firelight shone on the amethyst ring as Miss Ainslie moved it on her finger.

"He said that he would have no way of writing this time, but that, if anything happened, I would know. I was to wait—as women have waited since the world began.

"Oh, Ruth, do you know what waiting means? Mine has lasted through thirty-three interminable years. Each day, I have said: 'he will come to-morrow.' When the last train came in, I put the light in the window to lead him straight to me. Each day, I have made the house ready for an invited guest and I haven't gone away, even for an hour. I couldn't bear to have him come and find no welcome waiting, and I have always worn the colour he loved. When people have come to see me, I've always been afraid they would stay until he came, except with you—and Carl. I was glad to have you come to stay with me, because, lately, I have thought that it would be more—more delicate than to have him find me alone. I loved you, too, dear," she added quickly.

"I—I asked your aunt to keep the light in the window. I never told her why, but I think she knew, and you must tell her, dear, the next time you see her, that I thank her, and that she need never do it again. I thought, if he should come in a storm, or, perhaps, sail by, on his way to me——"

There was another long silence, then, with an effort, she went on. "I have been happy, for he said he wanted me to be, though sometimes it was hard. As nearly as I could, I made my dream real. I have thought, for hours, of the things we would say to each other when the long years were over and we were together again. I have dressed for his eyes alone, and loved him—perhaps you know——"

"I know, Miss Ainslie," said Ruth, softly, her own love surging in her heart, "I know."

"He loved me, Ruth," she said, lingering upon the words, "as man never loved before. In all of God's great universe, there was never anything like that—even in Heaven, there can't be anything so beautiful, though we have to know human love before we can understand God's. All day, I have dreamed of our little home together, and at night, sometimes—of baby lips against my breast. I could always see him plainly, but I never could see our—our child. I have missed that. I have had more happiness than comes to most women, but that has been denied me."

She leaned back in her chair and closed her eyes. Her lips were white and quivering, but there were no tears. At length she sat upright and fixed her eyes upon Ruth.

"Don't be afraid of anything," she said in a strange tone, "poverty or sickness or death, or any suffering God will let you bear together. That is n't love—to be afraid. There's only one thing—the years! Oh, God, the bitter, cruel, endless years!"

Miss Ainslie caught her breath and it sounded like a sob, but she bravely kept it back. "I have been happy," she said, in pitiful triumph; "I promised him that I would be, and I have kept my word. Sometimes it was hard, but I had my dream. Lately, this last year, I have often been afraid that—that something had happened. Thirty-three years, and you know, dear," she added, with a quaint primness, "that I am a woman of the world."

"In the world, but not of it," was on Ruth's lips, but she did not say it.

"Still, I know it was wrong to doubt him— I could n't, when I thought of our last hour together, out on the hill in the moonlight. He said it was conceivable that life might keep

him from me, but death never could. He told
me that if he died, I would know, that he
would come and tell me, and that in a little
while afterward, we should be together."

The dying embers cast a glow upon her face.
It was almost waxen in its purity; she seemed
transfigured with the light of another world.

"Last night, he came to me—in a dream.
He is dead—he has been dead for a long
time. He was trying to explain something to
me—I suppose he was trying to tell me why
he had not come before. He was old—an
old man, Ruth, and I have always thought of
him as young. He could not say anything
but my name—' Mary — Abby — Mary —
Abby—' over and over again; and, once,
'mother.' I was christened 'Mary Abigail,'
but I never liked the middle name, so I
dropped it; and he used to tease me sometimes by calling me 'Abby.' And—from
his saying 'mother,' I know that he, too,
wherever he may be, has had that dream of
—of our child."

Ruth was cold from head to foot, and her
senses reeled. Every word that Winfield had
said in the morning sounded again in her ears.
What was it that went on around her, of

which she had no ken ?   It seemed as though
she stood absolutely alone, in endless space,
while planets swept past, out of their orbits,
with all the laws of force set suddenly aside.

Miss Ainslie felt her shuddering fear.
"Don't be afraid, dear," she said again,
"everything is right. I kept my promise, and
he kept his. He is suffering — he is very
lonely without me; but in a little while we
shall be together."

The fire died out and left the room in darkness, broken only by the last fitful glow.
Ruth could not speak, and Miss Ainslie sat
quietly in her chair. "Come," she said at
last, stretching out her hand, " let 's go upstairs. I have kept you up, deary, and I
know you must be very tired."

The house seemed filled with a shadowy
presence — something intangible, but por-
tentous, for both good and ill. Ruth took
down the heavy mass of white hair and
brushed it back, tying it at the neck with a
ribbon, in girlish fashion, as Miss Ainslie
always did. Her night gown, of sheerest
linen, was heavy with Valenciennes lace, and
where it fell back from her throat, it revealed
the flesh, exquisitely white, set in gracious

curves and womanly softness, as if by a sculptor who loved his clay.

The sweet, wholesome scent of the lavender flowers breathed from the folds of Miss Ainslie's gown, as she stood there in the candle light, smiling, with the unearthly glow still upon her face.

"Good night, deary," she said; "you'll kiss me, won't you?"

For a moment the girl's face was buried among Miss Ainslie's laces, then their lips met. Ruth was trembling and she hurried away, swallowing the lump in her throat and trying to keep back the tears.

The doors were open, and there was no sound save Miss Ainslie's deep breathing, but Ruth kept a dreary vigil till almost dawn.

XVI

Some One Who Loved Her

THE summer waned and each day, as it slipped away, took a little of Miss Ainslie's strength with it. There was neither disease nor pain — it was simply a letting go. Carl sent to the city for a physician of wide repute, but he shook his head. "There's nothing the matter with her," he said, "but she does n't want to live. Just keep her as happy as you can."

For a time she went about the house as usual, but gradually, more and more of her duties fell to Ruth. Hepsey came in every day after breakfast, and again in the late afternoon.

Ruth tried to get her to go out for a drive, but she refused. "No, deary," she said, smiling, "I've never been away, and I'm too old to begin now." Neighbours, hearing of her illness, came to offer sympathy and help,

but she would see none of them — not even
Aunt Jane.

One night, she sat at the head of the table as
usual; for she would not surrender her place as
hostess, even though she ate nothing, and afterward a great weakness came upon her. "I
don't know how I'll ever get upstairs," she
said, frightened; "it seems such a long way!"

Winfield took her in his arms and carried
her up, as gently and easily as if she had been
a child. Her cheeks were flushed and her
eyes bright when he put her down. "I
never thought it would be so easy," she said,
in answer to his question. "You'll stay
with me, won't you, Carl? I don't want
you to go away."

"I'll stay as long as you want me, Miss
Ainslie, and Ruth will, too. We couldn't do
too much for you."

That night, as they sat in front of the fire,
while Miss Ainslie slept upstairs, Ruth told
him what she had said about leaving him the
house and the little income and giving her the
beautiful things in the house.

"Bless her sweet heart," he said tenderly,
"we don't want her things — we'd rather
have her."

"Indeed we would," she answered quickly.

Until the middle of September she went back and forth from her own room to the sitting-room with comparative ease. They took turns bringing dainties to tempt her appetite, but, though she ate a little of everything and praised it warmly, especially if Ruth had made it, she did it, evidently, only out of consideration for them.

She read a little, talked a little, and slept a great deal. One day she asked Carl to pull the heavy sandal wood chest over near her chair, and give her the key, which hung behind a picture.

"Will you please go away now," she asked, with a winning smile, "for just a little while?"

He put the bell on a table within her reach and asked her to ring if she wanted anything. The hours went by and there was no sound. At last he went up, very quietly, and found her asleep. The chest was locked and the key was not to be found. He did not know whether she had opened it or not, but she let him put it in its place again, without a word.

Sometimes they read to her, and she listened patiently, occasionally asking a question, but more often falling asleep.

"I wish," she said one day, when she was alone with Carl, "that I could hear something you had written."

"Why, Miss Ainslie," he exclaimed, in astonishment, "you would 'nt be interested in the things I write — it 's only newspaper stuff."

"Yes, I would," she answered softly; "yes I would."

Something in the way she said it brought the mist to his eyes.

She liked to have Ruth brush her hair, but her greatest delight was in hearing Winfield talk about her treasures.

"Won't you tell me about the rug, Carl, the one on the sandal wood chest?" she asked, for the twentieth time.

"It's hundreds of years old," he began, "and it came from Persia, far, far beyond the sea. The shepherds watched their flocks night and day, and saved the finest fleeces for the rug. They made colour from flowers and sweet herbs; from strange things that grew on the mountain heights, where only the bravest dared to go. The sumac that flamed on the hills, the rind of the swaying pomegranates, lichens that grew on the rocks by the Eastern sea, berries, deep-sea treasures, vine leaves, the juice of the grape — they all made colours for the rug, and then ripened, like old wine.

"After a long time, when everything was ready, the Master Craftsman made the design, writing strange symbols into the margin, eloquent with hidden meanings, that only the wisest may understand.

"They all worked upon it, men and women and children. Deep voices sang love songs and the melody was woven into the rug. Soft eyes looked love in answer and the softness and beauty went in with the fibre. Baby fingers clutched at it and were laughingly untangled. At night, when the fires of the village were lighted, and the crimson glow was reflected upon it, strange tales of love and war were mingled with the thread.

"The nightingale sang into it, the roses from Persian gardens breathed upon it, the moonlight put witchery into it; the tinkle of the gold and silver on the women's dusky ankles, the scent of sandal wood and attar of rose — it all went into the rug.

"Poets repeated their verses to it, men knelt near it to say their prayers, and the soft wind, rising from the sea, made faintest music among the threads.

"Sometimes a workman made a mistake, and the Master Craftsman put him aside. Often, the patient fingers stopped weaving forever, and they found some one else to go on with it. Sometimes they went from one place to another, but the frame holding the rug was not injured. From mountain to valley and back again, urged by some strange instinct, past flowing rivers and over the golden sands of the desert, even to the deep blue waters that broke on the shore — they took the rug.

"The hoof-beats of Arabian horses, with white-robed Bedouins flashing their swords; all the glitter and splendour of war were woven into it. Songs of victory, the rush of a cavalry charge, the faith of a dying warrior, even the slow marches of defeat—it all went into the rug.

"Perhaps the Master Craftsman died, but the design was left, and willing fingers toiled upon it, through the long years, each day putting new beauty into it and new dreams.

Then, one day, the final knot was tied, by a
Veiled Lady, who sighed softly in the pauses
of her song, and wondered at its surpassing
loveliness."

"And—" said Miss Ainslie, gently.

"Some one who loved you brought it to
you."

"Yes," she repeated, smiling, "some one
who loved me. Tell me about this," she
pleaded, touching a vase of Cloisonnè.

"It came from Japan," he said, "a strange
world of people like those painted on a fan.
The streets are narrow and there are quaint
houses on either side. The little ladies flit
about in gay attire, like so many butterflies—
they wear queer shoes on their dainty feet.
They're as sweet as their own cherry blossoms.

"The little man who made this vase, wore
a blue tunic and had no robes of state, because
he was poor. He loved the daughter of a
nobleman and she loved him, too, though
neither dared to say so.

"So he sat in front of his house and worked
on this vase. He made a model of clay,
shaping it with his fingers until it was perfect. Then a silver vase was cast from it and

over and over it he went, very carefully, making a design with flat, silver wire. When he was satisfied with it, he filled it in with enamel in wonderful colours, making even the spots on the butterflies' wings like those he had seen in the fields. Outside the design, he covered the vase with dark enamel, so the bright colours would show.

"As he worked, the little lady he loved came and watched him sometimes for a moment or two, and then he put a tiny bit of gold into the vase. He put a flower into the design, like those she wore in her hair, and then another, like the one she dropped at his feet one day, when no one was looking.

"The artist put all his love into the vase, and he hoped that when it was done, he could obtain a Court position. He was very patient with the countless polishings, and one afternoon, when the air was sweet with the odour of the cherry blossoms, the last touches were put upon it.

"It was so beautiful that he was commissioned to make some great vases for the throne room, and then, with joy in his heart, he sought the hand of the nobleman's daughter.

"The negotiations were conducted by another person, and she was forced to consent, though her heart ached for the artist in the blue tunic, whose name she did not know. When she learned that her husband was to be the man she had loved for so long, tears of happiness came into her dark eyes.

"The vase had disappeared, mysteriously, and he offered a large reward for its recovery. At last they were compelled to give up the hope of finding it, and he promised to make her another one, just like it, with the same flowers and butterflies and even the little glints of gold that marked the days she came. So she watched him, while he made the new one, and even more love went into it than into the first one."

"And—" began Miss Ainslie.

"Some one who loved you brought it to you."

"Yes," she repeated, smiling, "some one who loved me."

Winfield fitted a story to every object in the room. Each rug had a different history and every bit of tapestry its own tale. He conjured up an Empress who had once owned the teakwood chair, and a Marquise, with patches and powdered hair, who wrote love letters at the marquetry table.

He told stories of the sea shells, and of the mermaids who brought them to the shore, that some one who loved her might take them to her, and that the soft sound of the sea might always come to her ears, with visions of blue skies and tropic islands, where the sun forever shone.

The Empress and the Marquise became real people to Miss Ainslie, and the Japanese lovers seemed to smile at her from the vase. Sometimes, holding the rug on her lap, she would tell them how it was woven, and repeat the love story of a beautiful woman who had worked upon the tapestry. Often, in the twilight, she would sing softly to herself, snatches of forgotten melodies, and, once, a lullaby. Ruth and Carl sat by, watching for the slightest change, but she never spoke of the secret in her heart.

Ruth had the north room, across the hall, where there were two dressers. One of them had been empty, until she put her things into it, and the other was locked. She found the key, one day, hanging behind it, when she needed some things for Miss Ainslie.

As she had half expected, the dresser was
full of lingerie, of the finest lawn and linen.
The dainty garments were edged with real
lace — Brussels, Valenciennes, Mechlin, Point
d'Alencon, and the fine Irish laces. Sometimes there was a cluster of tucks, daintily
run by hand, but, usually, only the lace, unless there was a bit of insertion to match.
The buttons were mother of pearl, and the
button holes were exquisitely made. One or
two of the garments were threaded with
white ribbon, after a more modern fashion,
but most of them were made according to the
quaint old patterns. There was a dozen of
everything.

The dried lavender flowers rustled faintly
as Ruth reverently lifted the garments, giving
out the long-stored sweetness of Summers
gone by. The white had changed to an
ivory tint, growing deeper every day. There
were eleven night gowns, all made exactly
alike, with high neck and long sleeves,
trimmed with tucks and lace. Only one was
in any way elaborate. The sleeves were
short, evidently just above the elbow, and
the neck was cut off the shoulders like a ball
gown. A deep frill of Venetian point, with

narrower lace at the sleeves, of the same pattern, was the only trimming, except a tiny bow of lavender ribbon at the fastening, pinned on with a little gold heart.

When Ruth went in, with one of the night gowns over her arm, a faint colour came into Miss Ainslie's cheeks.

"Did — did — you find those?" she asked.

"Yes," answered Ruth, "I thought you'd like to wear them."

Miss Ainslie's colour faded and it was some time before she spoke again.

"Did — did you find the other — the one with Venetian point?"

"Yes, Miss Ainslie, do you want that one? It's beautiful."

"No," she said, "not now, but I thought that I'd like to wear that — afterward, you know."

A shadow crossed Ruth's face and her lips tightened.

"Don't, dear," said Miss Ainslie, gently. "Do you think he would think it was indelicate if — if my neck were bare then?"

"Who, Miss Ainslie?"

"Carl. Would he think it was wrong if I wore that afterward, and my neck and shoulders showed? Do you think he would?"

"No!" cried Ruth, "I know he wouldn't ! Oh, Miss Ainslie, you break my heart!"

"Ruth," said Miss Ainslie, gently; "Ruth, dear, don't cry! I won't talk about it any more, deary, I promise you, but I wanted to know so much!"

Ruth kissed her and went away, unable to bear more just then. She brought her chair into the hall, to be near her if she were needed. Miss Ainslie sighed, and then began to croon a lullaby.

XVII

Dawn

A S Miss Ainslie became weaker, she clung
to Carl, and was never satisfied when
he was out of her sight. When she was
settled in bed for the night, he went in to sit
by her and hold her hand until she dropped
asleep. If she woke during the night she
would call Ruth and ask where he was.

"He'll come over in the morning, Miss
Ainslie," Ruth always said; "you know it's
night now."

"Is it?" she would ask, drowsily. "I must
go to sleep, then, deary, so that I may be
quite rested and refreshed when he comes."

Her room, in contrast to the rest of the
house, was almost Puritan in its simplicity.
The bed and dresser were mahogany, plain,
but highly polished, and she had a mahogany
rocker with a cushion of old blue tapestry.
There was a simple white cover on the bed

and another on the dresser, but the walls
were dead white, unrelieved by pictures or
draperies. In the east window was a long,
narrow footstool, and a prayer book and
hymnal lay on the window sill, where this
maiden of half a century, looking seaward,
knelt to say her prayers.

One morning, when Ruth went in, she
said: "I think I won't get up this morning,
dear; I am so very tired. If Carl should
come over, will you say that I should like to
see him?"

She would see no one but Carl and Ruth,
and Mrs. Ball was much offended because her
friend did not want her to come upstairs.
"Don't be harsh with her, Aunt Jane,"
pleaded Ruth, "you know people often have
strange fancies when they are ill. She sent
her love to you, and asked me to say that she
thanked you, but you need not put the light
in the attic window any more."

Mrs. Ball gazed at her niece long and
earnestly. "Be you tellin' me the truth?"
she asked.

"Why, of course, Aunty."

"Then Mary Ainslie has got sense from
somewheres. There ain't never been no need

for that lamp to set in the winder; and when she gets more sense, I reckon she 'll be willin' to see her friends." With evident relief upon her face, Mrs. Ball departed.

But Miss Ainslie seemed quite satisfied, and each day spoke more lovingly to Ruth and Carl. He showed no signs of impatience, but spent his days with her cheerfully. He read to her, held her hand, and told her about the rug, the Marquise, and the Japanese lovers. At the end she would always say, with a quiet tenderness: "and some one who loved me brought it to me!"

"Yes, Miss Ainslie; some one who loved you. Everybody loves you; don't you know that?"

"Do you?" she asked once, suddenly and yet shyly.

"Indeed I do, Miss Ainslie—I love you with all my heart."

She smiled happily and her eyes filled. "Ruth," she called softly, "he says he loves me!"

"Of course he does," said Ruth; "nobody in the wide world could help loving you."

She put out her left hand to touch Ruth, and the amethyst ring slipped off, for her fingers were thin. She did not seem to notice when Ruth slipped it on again, and, shortly afterward, fell asleep.

That night Winfield stayed very late. "I don't want to leave you, dear," he said to Ruth. "I'm afraid something is going to happen."

"I'm not afraid—I think you'd better go."

"Will you put a light in your window if you want me, darling?"

"Yes, I will."

"I can see it from my room, and I'll be watching for it. If you want me, I'll come."

He awoke from an uneasy sleep with the feeling that Ruth needed him, and was not surprised to see the light from her candle streaming out into the darkness. He dressed hurriedly, glancing at his watch by the light of a match. It was just three o'clock.

Ruth was waiting for him at the lower door. "Is she—is she—"

"No, she seems to be just the same, but she wants you. She's been calling for you ever since you went away."

As they went upstairs Miss Ainslie's sweet voice came to them in pitiful pleading:

"Carl, Carl, dear! Where are you? I want you!"

"I'm here, Miss Ainslie," he said, sitting down on the bed beside her and taking her hot hands in his. "What can I do for you?"

"Tell me about the rug."

With no hint of weariness in his deep, quiet voice, he told her the old story once more. When he had finished, she spoke again. "I can't seem to get it just right about the Japanese lovers. Were they married?"

"Yes, they were married and lived happily ever afterward — like the people in the fairy tales."

"That was lovely," she said, with evident satisfaction. "Do you think they wanted me to have their vase?"

"I know they did. Some one who loved you brought it to you. Everybody loves you, Miss Ainslie."

"Did the Marquise find her lover?"

"Yes, or rather, he found her."

"Did they want me to have their marquetry table?"

"Of course they did. Did n't some one who loved you bring it to you?"

"Yes," she sighed, "some one who loved me."

She sang a little, very softly, with her eyes closed. It was a quaint old-fashioned tune, with a refrain of "Hush-a-by" and he held her hand until the song ceased and she was asleep. Then he went over to Ruth. "Can't you go to sleep for a little while, dearest? I know you're tired."

"I'm never tired when I'm with you," Ruth answered, leaning upon his arm, "and besides, I feel that this is the end."

Miss Ainslie slept for some time, then, all at once, she started as if in terror. "Letters," she said, very distinctly, "Go!"

He went to her and tried to soothe her, but failed. "No," she said again, "letters—Ruth —chest."

"She wants some letters that are in the sandal wood chest," he said to Ruth, and Miss Ainslie nodded. "Yes," she repeated, "letters."

Ruth went into the sitting-room, where a light was burning dimly, but the chest was locked. "Do you know where the key is, Carl?" she asked, coming back for a moment.

"No, I don't, dear," he answered. Then he asked Miss Ainslie where the key was, but she only murmured : "letters."

"Shall I go and help Ruth find them?"

"Yes," she said, "help—letters."

Together, they broke open the lock of the chest, while Miss Ainslie was calling, faintly : "Carl, Carl, dear ! Where are you ? I want you !"

"We'd better turn the whole thing out on the floor," he said, suiting the action to the word, then put it back against the wall, empty.

"We 'll have to shake everything out, carefully," returned Ruth, "that 's the only way to find them."

Wrapped carefully in a fine linen sheet, was Miss Ainslie's wedding gown, of heavy white satin, trimmed simply with priceless Venetian point. They shook it out hurriedly and put it back into the chest. There were yards upon yards of lavender taffeta, cut into dress lengths, which they folded up and put away. Three strings of amethysts and two of pearls slipped out of the silk as they lifted it, and there was another length of lustrous white taffeta, which had changed to an ivory tint.

Four shawls of Canton crepe, three of them
lavender and one ivory white, were put back
into the chest. There were several fans, of
fine workmanship, a girdle of oxidized silver,
set with amethysts and pearls, and a large
marquetry box, which contained tea.

"That's all the large things," he said; "now
we can look these over."

Ruth was gathering up great quantities of
lace—Brussels, Point d'Alencon, Cluny, Mechlin, Valenciennes, Duchesse and Venetian
point. There was a bridal veil of the Venetian lace, evidently made to match that on the
gown. Tiny, dried petals rustled out of the
meshes, for Miss Ainslie's laces were laid
away in lavender, like her love.

"I don't see them," she said, "yes, here
they are." She gave him a bundle of yellowed
letters, tied with lavender ribbon.

"I'll take them to her," he answered, picking up a small black case that lay on the floor,
and opening it. "Why, Ruth!" he gasped.
"It's my father's picture!"

Miss Ainslie's voice rose again in pitiful
cadence. "Carl, Carl, dear! Where are
you? I want you—oh, I want you!"

He hastened to her, leaving the picture in

Ruth's hand. It was an ambrotype, set into a case lined with purple velvet. The face was that of a young man, not more than twenty-five or thirty, who looked strangely like Winfield. The eyes, forehead and the poise of the head were the same.

The earth trembled beneath Ruth's feet for a moment, then, all at once, she understood. The light in the attic window, the marked paragraph in the paper, and the death notices—why, yes, the Charles Winfield who had married Abigail Weatherby was Miss Ainslie's lover, and Carl was his son.

"He went away!" Miss Ainslie's voice came again to Ruth, when she told her story, with no hint of her lover's name. He went away, and soon afterward, married Abigail Weatherby, but why? Was it love at first sight, or did he believe that his sweetheart was dead? Then Carl was born and the mother died. Twelve years afterward, he followed her —broken hearted. Carl had told her that his father could not bear the smell of lavender nor the sight of any shade of purple—and Miss Ainslie always wore lavender and lived in the scent of it—had he come to shrink from it through remorse?

Why was it, she wondered? Had he forgotten Miss Ainslie, or had he been suddenly swept off his feet by some blind whirlwind of passion? In either case, memory had returned to torture him a thousand fold — to make him ashamed to face her, with his boy in his arms.

And Aunt Jane knew of the marriage, at the time, probably, and said no word. Then she learned of Abigail Weatherby's death, and was still silent, hoping, perhaps, that the wanderer would come back, until she learned that Charles Winfield, too, was dead. And still she had not told Miss Ainslie, or, possibly, thought she knew it all till the day that Hepsey had spoken of, when she came home, looking "strange," to keep the light in the attic window every night for more than five years.

Was it kind? Ruth doubted for a moment, then her heart softened with love for Aunt Jane, who had hidden the knowledge that would be a death blow to Miss Ainslie, and let her live on, happy in her dream, while the stern Puritan conscience made her keep the light in the attic window in fulfilment of her promise.

As if the little light could reach the veil which hangs between us and Eternity, or penetrate the greyness which never parts save for a passage! As if all Miss Ainslie's love and faith could bring the dead to life again, even to be forgiven!

Her lips quivered when she thought of Miss Ainslie's tenderness for Carl and the little whispered lullabies that she sang to herself, over and over again. "She does not know," thought Ruth. "Thank God, she will never know!"

She put the rest of the things into the chest and closed it, covering it, as before, with the rug Miss Ainslie loved. When she went into the other room, she was asleep again, with her cheek pillowed on the letters, while Carl sat beside her, holding her hand and pondering over the mystery he could not explain. Ruth's heart ached for those two, so strangely brought together, who had but this little hour to atone for a lifetime of loss.

The first faint lines of light came into the eastern sky. Ruth stood by the window, watching the colour come on the grey above the hill, while two or three stars still shone dimly. The night lamp flickered, then went out. She set it in the hall and came back to the window.

As Miss Ainslie's rug had been woven, little by little, purple, crimson, and turquoise, gleaming with inward fires, shone upon the clouds. Carl came over to Ruth, putting his arm around her. They watched it together — that miracle which is as old as the world, and yet ever new.

"I don't see —" he began.

"Hush, dear," Ruth whispered, "I know, and I'll tell you some time, but I don't want her to know."

The sky brightened slowly, and the intense colour came into the room with the light. Ruth drew the curtains aside, saying, in a low tone, "it's beautiful, is n't it?"

There was a sudden movement in the room and they turned, to see Miss Ainslie sitting up, her cheeks flushed, and the letters scattered around her. The ribbon had slipped away, and her heavy white hair fell over her shoulders. Ruth went to her, to tie it back again, but she put her away, very gently, without speaking.

Carl stood by the window, thinking, and Miss Ainslie's eyes rested upon him, with wonder and love. The sunrise stained her white face and her eyes shone brightly, as sapphires touched with dawn. The first ray of the sun came into the little room and lay upon her hair, changing its whiteness to gleaming silver. Then all at once her face illumined, as from a light within.

Carl moved away from the window, strangely drawn toward her, and her face became radiant with unspeakable joy. Then the passion of her denied motherhood swelled into a cry of longing — "My son!"

"Mother!" broke from his lips in answer. He went to her blindly, knowing only that they belonged to each other, and that, in some inscrutable way, they had been kept apart until it was too late. He took her into his arms, holding her close, and whispering, brokenly, what only she and God might hear. Ruth turned away, sobbing, as if it was something too holy for her to see.

Miss Ainslie, transfigured with unearthly light, lifted her face to his. Her lips quivered for an instant, then grew cold beneath his own. She sank back among the pillows, with her eyes closed, but with yet another glory upon the marble whiteness of her face,

as though at the end of her journey, and beyond the mists that divided them, her dream
had become divinely true.

Then he, who should have been her son,
bent down, the tears falling unheeded upon
her face, and kissed her again.

THE END.